Laura Zigman grew up in Newtonville, Massachusetts, and graduated from the University of Massachusetts at Amherst. She spent ten years in New York City working in book publishing and currently lives in Washington, D.C. *Animal Husbandry* is her first novel.

Praise for *Animal Husbandry*

"A hilarious dissection of the mores of the male New Yorker . . . Laura Zigman's first novel, with its echoes of *Bridget Jones' Diary*, is a punchy and amusing read. It is a cruel exposé of male inadequacies and of the vast gulf that exists between male and female expectations." *Spectator*

"Fresh and hilarious . . . should do for dumped girlfriends what Olivia Goldsmith's *The First Wives Club* and Fay Weldon's *The Life and Loves of a She-Devil* did for dumped wives." *Time*

"A transatlantic *Bridget Jones' Diary* . . . *Animal Husbandry* will hit nerves with its blithely non-feminist world view. It will engage those who'd like to laugh at incurable romantics but have themselves suffered symptoms." *Independent on Sunday*

"A great read . . . hugely entertaining" *Prima*

"A hilarious contribution to the Bridget Jones school of literature" *Good Housekeeping*

"Sharp, sassy . . . an irresistibly entertaining read" *Ideal Home*

"A screwball romantic comedy" *Options*

"A tre⬚⬚⬚⬚⬚⬚⬚⬚y funny novel mercilessly expos⬚⬚⬚⬚⬚⬚⬚⬚⬚⬚nt-phobes" *Cosmopolitan*

ANIMAL HUSBANDRY

Laura Zigman

ARROW

Published in the United Kingdom in 1999 by Arrow Books

1 3 5 7 9 10 8 6 4 2

First published in the United Kingdom in 1998 by Hutchinson

Arrow Books Limited
Random House UK Ltd
20 Vauxhall Bridge Road, London, SW1V 2SA

Random House Australia (Pty) Limited
20 Alfred Street, Milsons Point, Sydney,
New South Wales 2061, Australia

Random House New Zealand Limited
18 Poland Road, Glenfield, Auckland 10, New Zealand

Random House South Africa (Pty) Limited
Endulini, 5a Jubilee Road, Parktown 2193, South Africa

Random House UK Limited Reg. No. 954009

A CIP catalogue record for this book is available from the British Library

Papers used by Random House UK Limited are natural,
recyclable products made from wood grown in sustainable forests.
The manufacturing processes conform to the environmental
regulations of the country of origin

Printed and bound in the United Kingdom by
Mackays of Chatham PLC, Chatham, Kent

ISBN 0 09 924852 2

This novel is a work of fiction. Names, characters, places, and incidents either are the product of the author's imagination or are used fictitiously. Any resemblance to actual persons, living or dead, events, or locales is entirely coincidental.

For my parents,
Bernie and Bernice

For my late grandmother,
Ruth Black

For Linda,
the best sister ever,

and for Wendy,
who made me finish.

·☾ ☽·

ANIMAL HUSBANDRY

·☽ ☾·

Darwinian Man, though well-behaved,
At best is only a monkey shaved.

—W. S. Gilbert
Princess Ida, Act II

PREFACE:
THE NEW-COW THEORY

By nature, man loves change. He is attracted by beauty, attracted by novelty. To this, the *Yoga Vasishtha* gives a philosophical reply: "From the moment one has obtained something desired, it is no longer desirable. The desire to obtain something disappears at the moment it is obtained."

The Kama Sutra

·☾ ☽·

IF SOMEONE HAD ASKED ME a year ago why I thought it was that men leave women and never come back, I would have said this:

New Cow.

New Cow is short for *New-Cow theory,* which is short for *Old-Cow–New-Cow theory,* which, of course, is short for the sad, sorry truth that men leave women and never come back because all they really want is New Cow.

The New-Cow theory was not my theory, though I re-named it and refined it for my own purposes. The seed of the New-Cow theory was culled from an article on male behavior that caught my eye, partly because it appeared in a highly reputable newspaper and not in a self-help book with a twenty-three-word title, and partly too, I think, because of the timing, which was about nine months after Ray had left me for no apparent reason and right after I found out that his no apparent reason had had a name all along:

New Cow.

The New-Cow theory was based on several seminal studies cited in the article on the mating preferences of the male cow.

First, a bull was presented with a cow.

They mated.

When the bull was presented with the same cow, to mate again, the bull wasn't interested. He wanted *New* Cow and this was *Old* Cow.

At which point the same cow was brought in again, only this time the researchers disguised her slightly—with a hat or a little dress. And again the bull refused to mate with her because he could tell that she wasn't New Cow. She was just Old Cow *dressed* as New Cow.

Finally, realizing the bull couldn't be tricked visually, an ingenious ploy was implemented: *The Old Cow was smeared with New-Cow scent.* Smelling New Cow, the bull got up and crossed the barn to get a better look.

But he was no fool. This wasn't New Cow.

This was Old Cow incognito.

Old Cow in sheep's clothing.

Mutton dressed as lamb.

If someone had asked me a year after Ray and I first met what I thought about why men leave women and never come back, I would have told them a lot of things to substantiate the New-Cow theory.

Like how some male insects hold out a big wet, gooey ball of food to lure a prospective female, then take the uneaten portion with them after copulation to use to attract another prospective female.

Or how the lag time between rats' erections can be significantly decreased when a new female is thrown into the cage.

And how the males of most species will attempt to copulate with almost anything that even remotely resembles a female: a male turkey with a female turkey head; a male snake with a dead female snake until redirected to a live one; a male bonobo with a cardboard box or a pretty zookeeper's big rubber boots.

Old Cows think they know everything about everything.

But no one asked me then.

If someone asked me now, I would have a different answer.

I would roll my eyes, look toward the ceiling, raise both

hands and shake them toward the heavens the way old Italian women do, and say this:

It is not for us to understand.

That's what people who have given up say, and, I suppose, I was one of those people. And maybe I had given up because I came to realize that men didn't leave all women and never come back.

They just left me.

My name is Jane Goodall.

Not *the* Jane Goodall, but sometimes I think it was my name that led me from men to cows, from cows to monkeys, and then to all my research and theories. Everything has meaning, no matter how seemingly random or insignificant; everything leads us to something else: a blink of an eye, a kiss, a facial expression, a particular combination of words, like *I don't love you anymore* or *I'm in love with someone else now,* are all clues to be deciphered, analyzed, interpreted. At least that's what I, Jane Goodall, monkey scientist, once believed.

But I am not a monkey scientist anymore.

I'm a *recovering* monkey scientist.

You'd think, with all the twelve-step recovery programs out there—with all the touchy-feely, all-embracing, anti-enabling groups of people meeting five times a day, hugging one another and telling one another their first names and their excessive-eating-smoking-drinking-drugging-fucking stories— that there would have been one for me. One measly, pathetic group of two or three equally obsessive-compulsive monkey scientists who would have listened to my sapien-simian rantings and understood.

But no. In order to rebuild my life—or, actually, in order to *get* a life—I had to quit my personal version of animal husbandry cold turkey.

I had to come up with my own recovery program.

I share it with you now, in its entirety, in case you might find it useful:

They will never make sense; you will never understand them.

INTRODUCTION:
THE OLD-COW STORY

In competitive bull-riding, the idea is to stay on for eight seconds and win the money. This is harder than it sounds, and when it doesn't work out, riders move to Plan B, which is to fall in the dirt and get away.

According to Ted Nuce, who rode about 175 bulls last year, even Plan B is harder than it sounds: "Bulls will come after you," Nuce said. "They don't just want to step on you. They want to run over top of you, or hook you. Their nature is to do that."

The Washington Post, October 1, 1996

·☾ ☽·

NOTHING MAKES another Old Cow cry more than a good Old-Cow story. *Their* Old-Cow story.

You start telling someone your tragic little tale—how Cow met Bull, or Bull met Cow, or Bull met Bull—and before you can get to the part about the hat and the little dress, they interrupt you and start telling you *their* story, and before you can say, "Hey, what about me?" they're waving for another drink and repeating what they were told when they were in your condition.

This is how it usually goes.

Broken hearts mend, they say.

Time heals all wounds, they say.

Have another Wild Turkey. Trust me, they say.

Then, when you don't trust them, and you won't, because you trusted before and all it got you was two fifty-minute sessions a week, you play with your straw and lean back from the table. Because here come the human body arguments, the parade of mending limbs, near-invisible incisions, minds learning to rewire themselves—tangible proof of the body's amazing ability to recover, to heal, to forget.

But you already know about those metaphors. You've watched the same science documentaries, sifted out the same small stones of truth. You know how bones bond stronger in the broken places, like glued dinner plates; how scars spread over split skin and fill in the cracks like soft spackle; how memories die slowly and quietly, taking their light with them like stars. They're the familiar rationalizations you once told others and now refuse to tell yourself.

When all else fails, which it will, because no one can trick you into parting with your pain for even an instant—*it's all you have left now, besides the shrink bills*—they pull out all the stops.

Time wounds all heels, they say.

Maybe he'll come back, they say.

I think I'll have another Wild Turkey, they say.

My God.

The things people will say to make themselves stop sobbing.

For me it was the word *time*.

At the beginning I tried to imagine what it would be like when time had passed and I was over Ray—at night when I couldn't sleep, I'd close my eyes and try to picture all those days and months, all the passing seasons and the changing light, rushing ahead like some time-lapse film clip.

But there are some leaps the mind can't make.

Those nights with my eyes closed I learned many lessons.

That kissing the perfect washboard stomach is not something you can be expected to forget overnight.

That there is a high-interest layaway payment plan for passion: one year of pain for every month of pleasure spent.

That most of the things men say turn out to be lies, even if they don't mean them to be, and even if they never admit it.

That there is something different in the eyes of lost-boy men—a certain sadness, a need, a tenderness—which can make you forgive them almost anything.

There was more.

I learned a lot that year after Ray left me.

Like how to tell my Old-Cow story without sounding too much like Glenn Close.

I can do that now, almost, after two years. And a hundred and ninety-two sessions.

There's not much good you can say about sensory-deprivation weekends and therapy except that they give you time to get your story straight.

I came up with several Old-Cow stories, actually, several different versions of the same truth that I could pick from, like wines, depending on my mood and the nature of my audience.

This was one:

Cow met Bull.

Cow and Bull mated.

Bull dumped Cow.

The *veni, vidi, vici* version was another:

Bull *met* Cow.

Bull *mated* Cow.

Bull *dumped* Cow.

This one was classified for my own case file:

Cow met Bull.

Cow thought Bull was attractive in a shy, muscular, fine-boned, J. Crew sort of way but assumed, since this was New York, that he liked Bulls too. So Cow did a little digging and found out that Bull did indeed like Cows—in fact, he had a Cow, a difficult and demanding vegetarian Heifer to whom he was engaged.

But while they were away on a business trip together, Bull told Cow how unhappy he was with his Current Cow—how they didn't really have much in common and how they barely mated anymore. Cow was intrigued, but she didn't get up and charge—she had heard this line before, and besides, given her last two experiences with emotionally enyoked males, there was her new golden rule: *No more Bulls with Cow complications.*

However, Cow liked the way Bull looked in his button-down shirts and ties and the way he was always pushing his wire-rimmed glasses back up his nose. She liked that he grew up on Long Island and that he rode his bicycle to work from the Upper West Side and that he wore the same dark-green rubber field coat every day. So a few weeks later, when Bull asked her to meet him for a drink, Cow got up and ambled toward the barn.

Like an idiot.

But I'm getting ahead of myself.

There are few things people distrust more in this world than an Old Cow's Old-Cow story, no matter which version it is, so I just want to say now, before I go any further, that I know you don't believe me.

You may want to; you may, in fact, believe that *I* believe what I'm saying is true, but inside, to yourself, I know what you're thinking.

That it was me.

That I did something wrong.

That it was my fault.

If by that you mean that I mistook lust for love, that he never loved me, that I was a fool, then perhaps you're right.

Maybe I did.

Maybe he didn't.

Maybe I was.

Sometimes I don't believe myself either.

But if you mean that it was my fault for misreading the situation—that if you had been me, you would have been able to tell the difference, that you would have been able to distinguish the lies from the truth, that you wouldn't have believed, to the depths of your soul, to the very core of your being, that this was, positively, unmistakably, at long last, *love*—then, for you I have a different version of my Old-Cow story, a version I didn't tell you about.

It's the one I almost never tell anyone—not even myself—anymore. It isn't glib and bitter and well rehearsed like the others, and, more importantly, it isn't tearproof. Sad, sorry truths almost never are.

Ray and I met.

I fell in love.

And for a brief moment in time, when he was in my life and I was in his, the world became a very different place.

And when he left, and when it was over, and when I realized, finally, that he was never, ever coming back, it broke my heart.

PRECOPULATORY PHASE: STAGE I
THE MYTH OF MALE SHYNESS

Some patients with narcissistic personalities present strong conscious feelings of insecurity and inferiority. At times, such feelings of inferiority and insecurity may alternate with feelings of greatness and omnipotent fantasies. At other times, and only after some period of analysis, do unconscious fantasies of omnipotence and narcissistic grandiosity come to the surface. The presence of extreme contradictions in their self concept is often the first clinical evidence of the severe pathology in the ego and superego of these patients, hidden underneath a surface of smooth and effective social functioning.

—Otto Kernberg, Ph.D.
Borderline Conditions and Pathological Narcissism

·☾ ☽·

LOOKING BACK NOW, of course, I can see that it wasn't just me who got dumped.

It was just one of those years.

We all became casualties of love, survivors of the same shots through the heart. We were all led down the garden path and left to crawl our way back from the middle of the jungle.

First David, my friend from college.

Then me.

Then my best friend, Joan.

And then there was my roommate, Eddie, the veteran of luv, the one with the post-traumatic stress disorder, wheeling around the proverbial ward and goosing all the nurses.

It was his apartment I moved into right after Ray dumped me.

And it was from living with Eddie—living inside the belly of the beast, as it were—that led me to my research. Because a woman doesn't just wake up one morning like something out of Kafka's *Metamorphosis,* a fully formed psycho, holding a *Portable Freud* in one hand and Darwin's *Origin of Species* in the other.

She doesn't just start reading *Black's Law Dictionary* or *The Diagnostic and Statistical Manual of Mental Disorders* one day, out of the blue, for pleasure.

She is driven to it.

Slowly.

Over time.

Like I was.

———

It all started when Ray and I were standing on First Avenue, late one Friday night at the end of June, after everyone else had gone home.

A few hours earlier he had called me from a bar in the East Village I had never heard of. "Hurry hurry," he had said over the noise, "or you'll miss *the hair*."

It was midnight.

I put the phone down and sat up in bed, shocked that he had called. As I'd left the office earlier that evening, he was standing with a few people talking about meeting up later for drinks to celebrate our boss's brief vacation. "You should come," he'd said. "It'll be fun."

Fun. My idea of fun most nights was going straight home from work and climbing into bed with a pile of back issues of *The New Yorker* and a bowl of Cheerios. Which is what I'd done that night since Joan was going to a screening and David was in like again.

"Maybe," I'd told Ray. But later, once I was in bed, it occurred to me that he had been nervous when he asked me for my number so that he could call me later in case I changed my mind, and I'd regretted being so offhand about his invitation.

At that moment I considered my situation: snug as a bug in a rug in the safety and quiet of my sensory-deprivation tank— a perfect but miniature studio in a prewar elevator building in the West Village, with built-in bookshelves and a working fireplace—and I shook my head.

Loser.

So I hurried.

Fifteen minutes later, when I found Ray at the bar, he took my arm.

"You should have seen it," he said, looking around, hoping it was still there. "There were these two things, standing straight out, like this," he said, holding a few strands of his own hair out by the ends. Then he made the silent-scream face with his mouth and his eyes opened wide behind his wire-rimmed glasses. "It was like—roach antennae."

It was dark and humid and almost quiet when we stood under the parking sign, under the light, trying to think of what to do next.

"We could have a nightcap," I think I said, thinking it was forward enough to show that I was interested but not so forward as to scare the shit out of him, thinking it was the kind of thing two coworkers did at three in the morning after everyone else had gone home.

Ray looked at me and smiled shyly. "I was hoping this would happen," he whispered.

Then he looked away, and I looked away, and we both started walking west.

That's how it started.

With a phone call.

With a nightcap.

With a hair imitation.

With *shyness*.

That's how it always starts.

(Let me just interrupt myself for a minute to dispel a myth—that men are shy.

Men are not shy.

They may *seem* shy, they may even act shy, at the beginning, with all their Uriah Heep hand-wringing and obsequious seeping, but they are not, by any stretch of the imagination, shy.

Trust me. You'll see.)

PRECOPULATORY PHASE: STAGE II
ATTRACTION

The [fruit fly mating] ritual begins with a step called orientation. The male, who needs no instruction in this process, stands facing the female, about 0.2 millimeter away. Then he taps her on the abdomen with a foreleg and follows her if she moves away. Next, he displays one wing and flutters it to execute his form of a "love song." Depending on the female's level of interest at this point, he may go back and repeat his actions. . . . Fruit flies will not mate unless the males have gone through this entire routine and the female has become receptive.

Scientific American, April 1995

·☾ ☽·

RAY AND I ACTUALLY STARTED shortly after we met at work.

I was booking talent for *The Diane Roberts Show,* a serious late-night David-Susskind-esque talk show taped in New York. When the show was picked up nationally by public television that January, the station moved Diane and her assistant Evelyn over first, along with Diane's treadmill. But when the exercise equipment didn't fit in her office, Diane insisted that her space be reconfigured so that there was ample room in her three-windowed office for herself, the treadmill, her rack of wool blazers and turtlenecks, and her cases of personal-size bottles of Volvic water, which she kept unrefrigerated—and, of course, Evelyn, whose cubicle just outside Diane's office was reduced by half in the process. A few weeks later they moved the rest of us out of our shabby, cramped offices on 57th Street and Ninth Avenue into the slightly less cramped but still shabby studios on 57th Street and Eighth Avenue.

"Isn't this *fab*ulous?" Diane gushed the first morning we were all together again, camped out on the floor of her office because the greenroom hadn't been painted green yet. Diane's hair had just been triple-processed to "Diane Sawyer blond," as she called it, and she still had her post-Christmas St. Bart's glow. She touched a few of us on the head as she shimmied excitedly across the floor on her way back to her desk chair.

"Now. Before we get started on this month's schedule, I want to introduce our new executive producer, Ray Brown." Diane looked expectantly around the office. "Ray?" She fondled the rim of her Volvic bottle and swiveled around in her chair. "Evelyn, where's Ray?"

Evelyn poked her blond head out from under the rack of blazers. "He's in the studio."

"Oh," Diane said. She swiveled again and touched the intercom button that connected her to the studio's control room and spoke into the speaker unit. "Ray," she said with Helen Gurley Brown flirtatiousness. "We're meeting now." She kept her finger on the button and smiled until she heard his voice through the static.

"Yes. I know," the voice said. "But unfortunately I'm tied up in about fourteen feet of videotape that just exploded out of its cassette."

Diane laughed. "Okay. Then say hello to everyone I've just introduced you to."

There was a pause.

"Hello," the voice said.

"Good-bye," said Diane.

And that was the first I heard of the man who would, months later, ruin my life.

After exploring our new space, I liked the fact that there were actual offices instead of cubicles and that there were windows—that opened. And the fact that half of the twenty-five people who worked there were men—and straight—and that all of them were good-looking wasn't too hard to take either.

Can you tell it had been a while since I'd been out on a date?

"No way," Joan had said enviously when I called to tell her about my first day. Joan and I had known each other since we were both assistants at *People* magazine sitting out in the same hallway, and we had never quite gotten over the thrill of having been promoted to windowed offices. Now she was an editor at *Men's Times* magazine and I was chasing down celebrities, and though neither of us had time to go to the bathroom once we got to the office, we still managed to talk to each other on the phone at least eleven times a day.

"It's true," I said, eyeing the painted mullions and pretending to enjoy a cold, damp breeze. "They open and everything."

Joan typed loudly into the phone. I imagined her thick dark hair exploding out of its ponytail the way it always did when it was rainy and humid. "I wasn't talking about the *windows,*" she said, annoyed. "I was talking about the *view.*"

Ray's office was down the hall and around the corner from mine, on the other side of the floor, next to Diane's office, and far enough away for me not to have much to do with him. As with most talk shows, people at my level reported to the executive producer. Diane, though, preferred that I report to her first and directly, so Ray and I had little direct contact on a day-to-day basis. All I knew about him then was that he was the new executive producer that PBS had assigned to us and that he drank a lot of coffee—information I had deduced from his ever-present clipboard and the thin fiber-optic microphones he wore around his neck like miniature stethoscopes, and from the number of times he passed by my office to and from the men's room (six times, on the average, before noon alone). That, and the fact that he had dark-brown hair, dark-brown eyes, and a soccer player's physique (my favorite combination of features) and an ass even a straight man would want to take a bite out of.

At the end of the first week he came into my office for the first time and handed me a memo.

"You don't have to read it," he said. "I write them so I won't get fired."

I took my glasses off and checked his face. His mouth moved into a wry smile, and when it did, one eyebrow went up, and I could see his teeth—big straight, bright-white teeth that momentarily fascinated me.

"I'm kidding. I wish I *would* get fired." He extended his hand and we shook. "I'm Ray Brown."

"I'm Jane Goodall."

"I know," he said. He looked around my office nervously and paced, stopping only to look at the two photographs tacked onto my bulletin board.

"Boyfriend?" he asked, pointing at the picture of David and me, taken the year before at a PBS fund-raiser when David still looked straight enough to trick people into thinking that he and I were dating.

"No," I said. "That's David. Just a friend."

"Just a friend," he repeated absently. Then he pointed at a strip of black-and-white pictures of Joan and me that we'd taken in a photo booth in the East Village. We went there together every year, on each of our birthdays, and this was the most recent strip, taken in late December, right after Joan had finally turned thirty too.

"Girlfriend? Significant other?"

I laughed and shook my head. "Practically. That's Joan. My best friend."

"You guys look alike," he said, still staring at the picture.

"I know. That's what happens when you spend too much time together."

Ray moved away from the bulletin board and back toward my desk. "So, that's a great name you have. People must comment on it a lot, I bet."

I nodded. "They always ask me if I'm into chimps."

He smiled. "And? Are you?"

"Not particularly. With the possible exception of Curious George when I was four."

"But Curious George was a monkey, not a chimp."

"There's a difference?"

"Big difference. You ought to know that with a name like yours. And since you don't, we should get the real Jane Goodall on the show. Fly her in from Tanzania or wherever the fuck she lives and educate you about your kin."

I laughed and then didn't say anything for a moment or two until I realized that he was still waiting for me to read his memo.

Due to the fact that Diane dislikes being touched by guests during the broadcast, please be advised that during all interviews guests will now be seated sixteen inches to Diane's left (i.e., out of arm's reach).

I put it down and looked at my arm. "Sixteen inches?" I said, making little inch measurements with my fingers. Then I looked at Ray. "Who touched her?"

"All the guests touch her. They like to take her hand while they're talking, or touch her on the arm. It makes them feel intimate, like they're close friends. Now that she thinks she's famous, she has this thing about everybody wanting something from her. It pisses her off."

"But I thought she liked that touchy stuff," I said. Since the show had gone national, Diane had gotten more relaxed, more casual, as if the show were being taped in the back booth of a bar at closing time. She'd even taken to wearing little black turtlenecks under her jackets, making her look like a short, perky, girlishly fifty David Susskind—or David Birney. "In fact," I said, "she's the one who always touches first."

"That's different," Ray said. "She's the host. It's her show."

Something wasn't adding up. I stared at Ray. "Who touched her?"

He hesitated, then smirked. "That guy from the World Bank. Two weeks ago. And it wasn't just her arm he was touching."

I laughed. I hadn't seen the show myself because of Diane's obsession with Kevin Costner. She had dispatched me that night to ambush him in the lobby of the St. Regis Hotel while he was in town promoting his new movie and to beg him to come on the show ("Give him a mug," she'd said, handing me a new one from the shelf behind her desk—a black glossy cup with THE DIANE ROBERTS SHOW in serious type on one side and a color headshot of herself on the other—"and tell him how much I loved *Wyatt Earp*."). But the next morning Carla, the associate producer, said that the World Bank segment looked like a grope fest.

"So sixteen inches is going to make a difference?"

"We measured," Ray said. "Some people's arms are longer than that, of course, but Diane seems to think that's the minimum distance to prevent unconscious touching. She thinks anything less than that makes it too easy."

"And what do you think?"

"I think it's ridiculous. I came from news. Two years with MacNeil/Lehrer. There was none of this handling-the-talent bullshit, no Macy's-Thanksgiving-Day-Parade-float-size egos. No chicken-neck-disguising black turtlenecks. No weighing themselves before tapings. Those guys sat there, read their stories, got up, and went home. The most I ever did was lend Jim a tie when he got it caught in his typewriter an hour before airtime. And I had to force it on him."

He walked over to the window and stood in front of the glass. Dusk had just started to fall, and I could see the sky turning pink behind the reflection of his face.

"Nice view," he said, tilting his head slightly and fixing his hair using the window's reflection. Then he checked his watch. "See you in the studio."

For sure.

Ray and I talked a few times after that in the following weeks, in the elevator, at the Xerox machine, in front of the building one Friday evening after a bright winter day that felt like spring. Once, in early March, we even went around the corner to the Carnegie Deli for lunch, and on the way there Ray helped an old woman across the street. I remember how impressed I was by his kindness when he stooped slightly and linked her arm through his.

"Please don't tell me you don't eat meat," Ray said when we sat down. He took his jacket off and pushed his menu away without looking at it.

I took my jacket off too and opened my menu. "I eat meat. Sometimes."

"Oh, Jesus. Thank God," he said. "I'm so tired of being looked at like an animal whenever I order something other than cheese." He signaled the waiter. "That's what happens when you're involved with a vegetarian. Sometimes I worry that she's going to follow me into a place like this and spray me with a can of red paint, like those wackos do to women wearing fur."

Here we go.

Enter: Current Cow.

"What does she do, your girlfriend?"

"My fiancée, actually." He took a sip of water. "Mia's a good-doer. Or do-gooder. Assistant director of an abortion clinic, by day, women's shelter volunteer by night."

I nodded. I didn't know what to say. On the basis of that mere two-sentence description she sounded humorless and self-righteous; someone I'd probably hate on sight but secretly envy later.

"Between her hours and my hours we almost never see each other except for weekends. Assuming there's no tofu rally or abortion convention." Curiously, he didn't sound too disappointed.

Amendment: Enter Current Cow with politically correct complications.

The waiter arrived. "Pastrami on rye," Ray announced with pride, patting his nonexistent gut. "Lots of mustard. And a big vanilla milkshake."

Boys.

Shiksa boys.

I ordered a tuna sandwich. On toast. Very ladylike.

Ray made a face. "Oh, *come* on."

I closed the menu. The waiter tapped his pencil. I looked at Ray and smirked. "Okay. I'll have what you're having. Without the milkshake."

"So tell me," he said, once the waiter had walked away. "How did you get into television?"

I sat back in the booth and thought a minute. "By accident. The way everyone in New York ends up doing what they're doing, probably: a lucky break from a temp job." I opened my big black bag (in New York, the bigger and blacker the accessory, the better) and put my sunglasses back in their case. "I was living in Princeton with my then-boyfriend, who was getting his Ph.D. in physics, and I was trying, with my pathetic little minor in art history, to get a job at one of the museums in the city. So I started temping, thinking I'd work for a year or two before going to graduate school too. One of my temp jobs was working for an assistant managing editor at *People* magazine, and because I typed a hundred words a minute, back when there were still typewriters, he begged me to stay. And that's where Joan and I met."

Ray's milkshake came, and he took a big gulp of it, sans straw. He wiped off the milkshake moustache and pushed the glass toward me. "Have some," he ordered. "It'll coat your stomach, protect it from *the meat*." So I did.

"Anyway," I continued, "I graduated from assistant to assistant editor, then associate editor. After six years there, not really writing but essentially 'producing' stories—spying, begging, tracking down handlers, coordinating everything so that the piece would coincide perfectly with whatever movie-book-video-CD-funeral-birth-wedding diet it was pegged to, I had this incredible Rolodex. One of those huge double-wheel ones that loomed on my desk like that big black thing in *2001*. I got tired of it, though, all that chasing around every week, the traveling, the deadlines, and I started thinking of getting it over with and applying to graduate school. But I didn't even know what I wanted to go back to school for. So when I heard about Diane's show starting up, I thought it would be a good compromise—something different but Rolodex applicable. Serious place. Serious interviews. *Issues*. A paycheck while I figured out what I really wanted to do with my life."

Ray nodded knowingly. "Less star-fucking."

"Little did I know that Diane lived to star-fuck."

Our sandwiches came, and for a few seconds neither of us spoke because our mouths were full.

"So whatever happened to the physicist?" Ray said finally.

I wiped a big yellow smear of mustard off my thumb onto my napkin. "Who?"

"Your boyfriend. The one you were living with in Princeton."

"Oh. Sorry." I chewed quickly. "Yeah, well, you know. Nothing. We'd been together for two years in college and then that year in Princeton, and, I don't know, it just didn't work out." The understatement of the millennium. Michael's incessant pushing me to go to graduate school too and my not wanting to stick around to find out exactly what was going on with him and his unnervingly attractive research partner made me make the move to Manhattan, where I never really believed I'd end up and where I'd certainly never planned on staying. But I did end up there, and I had stayed, and now, seven years later, I was still killing time.

Trying not to let the gaze of an incredibly handsome Bull interfere with the digestion that was supposed to be taking place in my four-compartment New-Cow stomach.

"How did we start talking about this?" I said and pushed my plate away.

"I asked you where you came from. How you got here. How you ended up in this place, having lunch with me." I glanced at Ray, and when our eyes met, I felt my heart race. He put his elbows on the table and rested his chin in his hands and looked right at me. "What?" he said softly. "What are you thinking?"

You mean, what am I thinking about besides your Current Cow?
My heart raced again. I loved it when men asked me what I

was thinking even though I was never sure how to answer them. I couldn't tell if they really wanted to know what I was thinking, or if they just wanted to make it look like they wanted to know. It was one of the gazillion questions I asked myself during moments like that, rare moments when I was sitting across from a man who was looking at me, waiting for me to speak; those split seconds every few years when the world seemed to stop and there was no noise in it, just the sound of my own breathing as I looked at a man's face and wondered what lay behind it, and what would happen next.

"I don't know," I said. "I guess I was thinking that it's been a long time since I thought about all that." Which was only partially true. I was thinking that it felt like all of it had happened a lifetime ago, that I had been a completely different person; and that I had no more idea of who I was then, at twenty-three, than of who I was now, at thirty.

When I got back to my desk, I called Joan.

"So I had lunch with this guy."

"What guy?"

"A guy. From here."

"Which guy from there?"

"Ray. The executive producer."

"Cute?"

"Very."

"Care to elaborate?"

"Tall. Dark. Thick, straight, longish hair. J. Crew type but not as Waspy."

Joan paused. I could tell she was scanning her mental hard drive left over from *People* to come up with the perfect celebrity quasi look-alike.

"Jimmy Smits but not Latino?"

"No."

"Andy Garcia but preppier?"

I thought a minute. "Yes, actually. Kind of."

"Hmm. Age?"

"Our age. Early thirties, I think."

"Marital status?"

"Uhm. . . . Engaged."

"Engaged." There was a pause. "Jane?"

"What?"

"Then, why are you calling me?"

I paused. "To ask you what I should wear to the wedding?"

Okay. Then I called David. Even invited him to dinner.

I always asked David about men I was interested in, not only because he was just as hopelessly attracted to attractive men as I was but because attractive men were his business. He was a freelance fashion photographer whose most recent credit was a men's underwear bus-ad campaign for a knock-off version of Calvin Klein briefs and boxers called Boy's Shorts, and as such he had become a keen observer of what made pretty boys tick. Being a pretty boy himself—just over six feet tall with a biweekly maintained edgy crew cut and a thrice-weekly pumped body—gave him an added advantage in understanding the male psyche. Which was why, over the years since college, where we had met, I had come to rely on his intuition and instincts in these situations more than my own.

"Hmm," David said later that night at the Sheridan Square diner. He lived around the corner from me on Bleecker Street, and the diner was around the corner from him. I'd arrived first and secured a booth by the window, and a few minutes later I saw him walking down the sidewalk with a guy I'd never seen before but who could have been his twin—both of them were wearing black leather car coats, white T-shirts, baggy pants, and big black Army boots. When he came in, he kissed me on the cheek and slid into the booth and then ordered a Greek salad. I ordered a bagel and coffee since my stomachs were still busy digesting my lunch.

"I don't know." He made a face and spit an olive pit into his hand. "Girlfriend, maybe. But"—he made the face again—"fiancée?"

"Yeah, but he makes all these disparaging remarks about her."

"Then you should wonder about him."

"Okay," I said. "You're right. It's stupid."

He wiped his mouth and finished his glass of water. "It's not stupid. It's just complicated."

"Too complicated, probably."

"Maybe. But maybe not. If you really like him, if you think you could really feel something for him, it might be worth trying for. I mean, he's not married yet." He picked up the check and put down a ten and a five. "My treat," he said, refusing to take my money. "So how do you feel about him?"

I wasn't sure, suddenly. "I barely know him. I mean, what can you know about someone after just one lunch?"

"You can know a lot. You can know how you feel." He stared at me and laid out a few singles when the waiter returned with the change. "So how do you *feel,* Jane? Do you like him? Do you like being with him? Do you feel happy when you're talking to him?"

I nodded.

"Then, why not try?"

I considered the question. "Because," I said finally. "I'm

tired of things that are this hard. This would be too hard. It would take too much work, and even if something did happen and it was great, he'd probably marry her anyway."

So I decided it was best to leave it alone. Leave Ray alone. Which, after a few days, wasn't as hard as I'd thought it would be. As the weeks passed, the show got busier and busier. With our new national profile it was easier getting the guests we wanted, and harder getting rid of the ones we didn't.

"Who booked Brooke Shields?" Diane asked one morning during a planning meeting in the greenroom, which was where the guests waited at night before their interviews and where the staff met during the day for meetings like this and cups of coffee and harried half-smoked cigarettes. Ray sat at the small rectangular Formica table across from Diane and across from Evelyn, who took the minutes. I sat next to him and next to Eddie, Diane's private detective–style researcher, who no one ever wanted to sit next to during meetings because he refused not to smoke.

Eddie was tall and rangy and rugged ("like an unshaven slightly dissipated Harry Hamlin," Joan had decided after meeting him at our office Christmas party), and though he and I had worked together for six months and had offices right next to each other, we'd barely spoken. All I knew about him was that he came to work most mornings well after eleven, smoked incessantly, always looked tired and depressed, and, according to office legend, was a womanizer—all of which apparently had something, if not everything, to do with a serious girlfriend who had left him.

Eddie looked at me, and I looked Carla, and Carla looked at Evelyn, and Evelyn looked at Ray, and then they all looked at Diane except for me.

"I did," I said finally, confessing my heinous crime. "I booked Brooke Shields."

Diane took a swig of her Volvic water. "Why? I think she's a loser. She's B list. We're not B list anymore. We're A list now. And we need A-list guests. A+-list guests."

"I know," I said. "It's just that last year we canceled her twice because of scheduling conflicts—and now, because we're national and because a play she's in is just about to open, her publicist called in the chit."

Diane stared at me—her chief talent booker, who'd just admitted she'd been worn down by some twelve-year-old publicist—and before I could think of what to say next, Eddie lit a cigarette and cleared his throat.

"I think Brooke Shields is cute."

There was silence for a few seconds, and then everyone started laughing. Even Diane. I turned to Eddie in disbelief and gratitude: Out of nowhere he'd come to my rescue and saved my ass.

"Thanks," I whispered.

Eddie graciously responded by blowing a long stream of smoke in my face. Then he grinned and leaned toward me almost imperceptibly. "You owe me," he said under his breath. "Big time."

At the end of May, Diane sent me down to Washington to scout for prospective guests at the annual book publishers' convention, and at the end of the first day, on Saturday, Ray showed up unexpectedly with Evelyn. It was almost three o'clock when they arrived on the convention floor, wearing shorts and T-shirts and fake badges, and when I asked him, he told me that they had decided to drive down at the last minute because Evelyn was going anyway to visit her parent, who lived nearby, and because he hadn't been to Washington for a while. It made me wonder whether the office scuttlebut about their being involved, fiancée notwithstanding was really true. But then he said, "If you're free later, after I drop Evelyn off, we could go to the Mall and see the sights," and I wasn't so sure.

I looked past him at Evelyn's long tan legs and shoulder-length horse hair, and tried not to think about my humidity induced frizzball hair or about what his invitation might mean.

"Okay," I said. I had never seen the Mall at night.

"Isn't this amazing?" he said. "The scope of it? The expansiveness of it? The *manifest destiny* of it?"

It was around eight o'clock that evening, and we were standing in front of The Gap, on the third level of the Pentagon City Mall, as it turned out. Ray strode into the store and over to a table of folded khakis. He held a pair by the waistband up to his stomach, and the pants dropped down, hitting his legs just above the ankles.

"Do you think they're too short?" he said, looking at me over the wire rims of his glasses.

He was like a kid, with his glasses, and his hair falling into his eyes, and his flood-level test-pants, but when he pulled up his T-shirt to reposition the waistband, I saw a ripple of abdominal muscles that made my mouth water.

I think I nodded.

"Good," he said, taking one last look and then refolding them. "If my pants aren't short, I trip over them."

Still salivating from the flash of flesh I had seen, I followed him stupidly as he headed toward the register. "I love to shop," he said, taking his wallet out of his back pocket. "I find it very comforting, the idea of being able to satisfy a need so easily.

Like now: I came down here with only an extra pair of boxer shorts and I needed a pair of pants—and now I have them." He looked at me and grinned. "Everything should be this easy. Mia thinks I'm insane. She thinks men are supposed to hate shopping. But I can't help it. I grew up on Long Island—Mall Country."

He paid for the pants with a credit card, then slipped the card and receipt into his wallet and slid the bag off the counter.

Mia again. I considered ignoring this second reference to her, but something—*New-Cow hormones?*—made me decide to take him by the horns and find out what the deal was.

"So. When's the wedding?" I said, my talk-show-producer guest-preinterview skills kicking in—asking direct, to-the-point questions you really don't want to know the answer to but that you need to know the answer to.

"When?" Ray slung the bag of pants over his shoulder and stared into the window of Williams-Sonoma. There were wicker picnic baskets bursting with long-stemmed champagne flutes and red-checkered tablecloths, and he eyed them suspiciously. "Is May National Picnic Month? If it is, maybe Diane'll want to do a show on that. You know, get a few retail gurus together. Maybe add Faith Popcorn. Talk about *trends*."

I stared into the window too but noticed only our reflection in it: one tall; the other short. One J.-Crew-model-bone-structure endowed; the other Semitically challenged. It felt strange suddenly to be shopping, together, in a mall, in another city, when we'd never been outside the studio except for that lunch. I saw him roll his eyes and turn away from the window, and then we started walking again.

"When am I getting married? I don't know, actually. Sometime next year. We haven't quite figured it out." He looked at me. "Do you think that's weird?"

Of course it was weird. "I don't know you well enough to know if it's weird or not."

"Well, it probably is. Most people who are getting married usually know when they're getting married." He smiled, and we kept walking.

"How did you meet?" I asked.

"At a friend's party in Montauk. I was about to start my master's in American history at Stanford. Mia had just graduated from Barnard, and I guess the thought of driving cross-country to San Francisco appealed to her. Which appealed to me." He looked down at his feet. "I guess I've always been shocked when someone shows the slightest bit of interest in me." He slung the Gap bag down off his shoulder and carried it in front of him like a small child. "Anyway, so we did, and we found this great apartment, the top floor of this big old house, and it was bliss for the first few years, but then, I don't know, something changed. I had this shitty legal proofreading job at night to help pay for tuition, and Mia started working at some rape crisis center, after which she stopped talking to me and stopped sleeping with me, and I would bike twenty miles a day, in the hills, down to the water, trying to figure out why I was with her. Now it's six years later and I'm still trying to figure that out."

I looked away. Even then I knew enough not to say anything negative about a man's girlfriend—past or present—no matter how much he seemed to want me to. Or, in Ray's case, how much he seemed to be begging me to. Sooner or later it always backfired.

"She's not an easy person," Ray continued. "I mean, she's a

vegan." He laughed and took his glasses off. "I don't know. Maybe I like being berated. Maybe I'm just naturally obsequious."

"Well, you must get something from each other," I said. "People don't usually stay together for no reason."

"It's not that we don't love each other," he clarified, which was surprising given what he'd just said. "We do. Just never at the same time." He rubbed his eyes and put his glasses back on. "Only now, we're practically like brother and sister. Sometimes it just seems harder to leave than to stay."

(*Better a Bull has some Cow than no Cow at all.*)

We walked through a set of automatic sliding doors and into the dark, humid air. Ray looked at me and elbowed me lightly. "So what about you? Were you ever going to get married without knowing exactly when you were going to get married?"

"Me? No." I smiled. "I came close once, but not since." Not since Michael.

"Why not?"

"I don't know," I said. Michael was not exactly parking-lot conversation.

"Oh, come on. I just told you my embarrassingly pathetic tale of woe, so you have to tell me yours."

I thought a minute. If I told, I risked sounding like a loser. If I didn't tell, I risked sounding like an *uptight* loser. "I drove cross-country too, the summer after the physicist and I met at Brown. In a Toyota station wagon with a hundred and thirty-six thousand miles on it. Michael—that was his name—was very into science, obviously, so we went to AAA and got all these maps. Maps of the entire United States, maps of the Northeast, the Southeast, the Midwest, the Southwest, the West Coast, the Northwest. Trip-tik maps with spiral bindings that showed every inch of road and had little symbols that stood for rest stops and bathrooms and gas stations.

"I had just learned to drive a standard, and after I'd fuck up my two-hour shift, Michael would take the wheel and make me get the Hewlett-Packard calculator out of the glove compartment and turn around in my seat and get the bags of maps out of the back to figure out the average number of rest stops that had bathrooms *and* gas stations. Then I'd get carsick from turning around, and then I'd divide wrong, and then we'd fight all the way to the next Rock Formation National Park and he'd lock me out of the car. He locked me out at Yosemite, at Yellowstone, and somewhere in the Badlands. Then we lived together for three more years. And somewhere in between all that I stopped sleeping with him too."

He shook his head empathetically as we reached the car. "God. I wonder what that would feel like," Ray said wistfully, looking up at the sky. "To really get along with the person you're with. I wonder if that's actually possible."

I looked up at the sky too. It was clear and black and full of stars. "Probably," I said, but the word came out sounding fake and halfhearted, like an unconvincing white lie. And as I looked at him, then at the little lines etched in the skin on either side of his mouth, I wondered, for the first time in a long time, when it was that I had stopped believing in the possibilities of things.

It hadn't happened overnight.

Those things never do.

Hope erodes slowly, over time, until you wake up one night

at three o'clock in the morning and realize: *I am not meant for that kind of thing.*

That kind of thing:

Romance.

Passion.

Being the object of someone's desire.

Showing up in someone else's dreams.

There had, of course, been men who had liked me, who had even loved me—men I'd been friends with and never slept with had told me so, months or even years later; men I'd slept with and never been friends with had told me too, sometimes, afterward. And obviously Michael had been in love with me once, at the beginning—before he knew that I'd never fully grasp the basic principles of particle physics—but never like that. Never enough.

Which, I suppose, made Michael and me equal in at least that one regard, since I had never been in love with him like that either.

But sometime after they had all left me to go back to their lives, their wives, to new women in whom they presumably saw what they hadn't seen in me—some spark of promise, some reflection of themselves they had never seen before but had always imagined seeing, some vision of their future—I would ride out the varying waves of crushing disappointment or secret relief until I came to assume that I was missing some element, some particular, elusive, intangible, crucial quality that made other women keepers. I didn't know exactly what that quality was, but I suspected it had something to do with clarity, with a lack of ambivalence, with the certainty of knowing what kind of relationship you wanted enough to be willing to try to get it. But after Michael and after a long string of short-term attachments—some intense, some not so intense; some bad, some not so bad—I was less sure about what I wanted than what I didn't want:

I didn't want to spend the rest of my thirties imprisoned in my office.

I didn't want to have to accept the idea that I might never have children.

And I didn't want to think about the fact that I might never find a soul mate.

Like Ray. Maybe.

Not that I thought that yet.

And not that he was such a prize either.

He was *engaged,* after all, and therefore, technically, unavailable.

And although he was smart and funny and tall and not Jewish, and even though I liked his mouth and his teeth and especially his hands—even the left one, the one with the imitation wedding band firmly embedded on the ring finger—he wasn't really my type.

Not really.

Not the type I'd always been attracted to and that had always been attracted to me.

Perpetually depressed.

Emotionally damaged.

Slightly secretive.

Desperate to be loved.

Desperate to be saved.

No, Ray was none of those things, and he displayed none of the usual neurotic psychopathic behaviors that initially ignited my imagination, my curiosity, my rescuer fantasies; that made me want to rip off the veil of his psyche and find out what lonely monster lurked underneath.

Ray, it seemed to me at the time, had no veil; he was just some above-normal average guy, a little obsessed with and unsure of himself, who seemed slightly, vaguely, improbably interested in me.

PRECOPULATORY PHASE: STAGE III
THE METAMORPHOSIS OF COW
TO NEW COW AND THE ROLE OF
THE CURRENT-COW SOB STORY

A prerequisite of love is that a man's face, at first sight, should reveal something to be respected, and something to be pitied.

—Stendhal, *Love*

·☾ ☽·

IN THE METAMORPHOSIS from Cow to New Cow, the Current-Cow sob story is an important phase.

This, of course, is when a man "accidentally" lets it slip out how unhappy he is with his Current Cow while he is ostensibly telling you some innocent and charmingly revealing story about himself and his past.

Sometimes confused with the almost identical Poor-Guy sob story, the Current-Cow sob story is so full of intimate Good-Bull–Bad-Cow details that it will seem completely believable—and even romantic—so much so that you will immediately find yourself in the throes of a full-blown crush and forget about one very important detail:

The Current Cow.

Allow me to deconstruct the essential elements:

1. *I know we just met, but did I happen to mention how sad, miserable, misunderstood, and lonely I've been my whole life?*

This is crucial to introducing the myth of male shyness and the Poor-Guy persona—common disguises for a wolf in sheep's clothing.

2. *You're so easy to talk to—not like my Current Cow.*

While you will think he is flattering you by trusting you with his life story, he is actually busy flattering himself by showing off how open, honest, and sensitive he is.

3. *I am not the asshole. She is, poor thing.*

Just in case you're starting to think he is a coldhearted, home-wrecking womanizer, *don't be so quick to judge,* because his description of her wounding inattention and indifference will prove that he is putting the Current Cow out to pasture for good reason and that he is tormented by guilt at the thought of abandoning her.

4. *What's that thing they always say about the love of a good woman (hint, hint)?*

That it can save a man from drowning. This is your cue to put the little white cap on and get the life preserver out of storage. *You're going on another rescue mission, Florence Nightingale.*

5. *Do I hear bells ringing?*

Yes, he does. And so should you. *New-Cow bells.* The empty barn beckons, the Bull awaits, so don't bother with the Old-Cow hat and red-lace Merry Widow. *You won't need them—yet.*

It was three weeks after Washington that Ray called me from the East Village. That night, after the hair, after the nightcap, after we got to Charles Street and climbed the four flights of stairs to my apartment and made coffee, we climbed two more flights to drink it on the roof and watch the sun come up.

"I can't remember the last time I did this," I said, "staying up all night talking with a virtual stranger." I looked down onto Bleecker Street and beyond to the Hudson River, feeling completely awake even though I'd barely touched my coffee. Whenever the last time was, it had been a long time—a very long time—since I'd felt that . . . happy.

Ray sat on the ledge of the roof with his back to the skyline and stretched his legs out. "I don't think I've ever done this before."

"Oh, come on. You probably do it all the time. Lure an unsuspecting woman out of her apartment at midnight to see some hair. Hint around after all the bars and diners within walking distance have closed until she invites you over for coffee."

"Then bore her with my entire life story until the sun rises and there's nothing left to do but watch cartoons."

"Cartoons?" I said.

"It's Saturday morning."

It was after seven when we went downstairs and sat on the bed, in the blue light, with the television on. Twice Ray got up to adjust the color/tint setting and each time he came back, it seemed he sat just an inch or two closer. But a little while later, at the end of Bugs Bunny, he turned to me and said: "You must be tired. Maybe I should go home and let you get some sleep."

And before I could turn to him and tell him that I wasn't tired, and that I didn't want him to go home, he took my hand. He didn't let go, and I didn't let go, and later, after he kissed me and told me that he'd wanted to do that from the first moment we'd met, I remembered what a small miracle it was to like someone and have them like you back.

[MATING SCENE DELETED.]

POST-COPULATORY PHASE: STAGE I
THE ESTABLISHMENT OF INTIMACY

What are the clinical characteristics of erotic desire as they become manifest in the course of psychoanalytic exploration? [One] is a search for pleasure, always oriented to another person, an object to be penetrated or invaded or to be penetrated or invaded by. It is a longing for closeness, fusion, and intermingling that implies both forcefully crossing a barrier and becoming one with the chosen object.

—Otto Kernberg
Love Relations: Normality and Pathology

·☾ ☽·

I THOUGHT we would leave it at that.

At a "small miracle."

At "like."

After he left that morning—after I'd replayed and analyzed everything that had just happened, I spent half the day dementedly imagining what it would be like if Ray and I got married. Then, when I couldn't get Joan on the phone, I called David, and spent the rest of the day at his apartment preparing what I would say when Ray came into my office on Monday morning for the Talk—the awkward, meandering, polite retraction of a "confused" man trying to get himself out of something he'd "accidentally" gotten himself into.

"Okay," I said, sitting down on David's couch. "So, like, I go to the office. And then I see him."

"Right," David said. He'd made coffee and poured us each a cup, then sat down in the armchair next to me. David had been in therapy for almost as long as I'd known him—long enough to treat me.

"Right." I nodded my head.

David nodded too. "In essence, then, you see each other."

"Right." We'd *see each other*.

He brought his cup up to his mouth with both hands and blew at the steam. "It might help if you imagine exactly where this would happen. Like, at the reception desk."

"Yes. Good," I said. Then I said nothing. I could feel the autism setting in again, and so could David. I put my head down on the pillow and stared at his foot.

"Jane?"

I craned my head so I could see him.

"This really isn't that hard." But obviously, from my lack of response, it was. "So he's there, and you're there, and then Ray says something like—and I'm going out on a limb here— 'Hello.' And you say?"

I took hold of his shoelace and pulled. "Hello?" I sat up on the couch and reached for my coffee. "But how do I say it? I mean, am I friendly? Aloof? Embarrassed? Unfazed? What's my motivation?"

"What's your motivation?" He ran his hand over the short, short hair on the back of his head and sighed loudly. "Jane, Jane, Jane-Jane-Jane. Why are you being so retarded?"

He waited, and when I said nothing, he came over and put his hands on my shoulders and bent his head to mine.

"Oh, I forgot," he said softly. "You always act this retarded when you really like someone."

But Ray did not leave it at that. And I was grateful not to have to wait until Monday to try out my big hello line.

"I hope I'm not bothering you," he said late on Sunday afternoon when he rang my doorbell unexpectedly, "but I just happened to be in the neighborhood."

Bothering me?

I opened the door, and he walked past me down the long, narrow hallway to the living room. He was wearing a baseball cap on frontward, an old gray Champion sweatshirt, basketball sneakers without socks, and a pair of khakis like the ones he'd bought in Washington, and when he leaned up against the wall, it occurred to me how good my apartment suddenly looked with him in it.

"I hope you like donuts," he said, walking over to me and opening the white paper bag he was holding so I could see inside. But I wasn't looking at the bag, and neither was he, and before I could think of something clever to say, he moved closer and kissed me twice.

"I can't stay. I'm house-sitting my friend's apartment and I forgot to feed the cats today." He looked at me and then away. "I guess I've been a little preoccupied."

"Me too."

"So. I was thinking maybe, tonight, if you wanted, you could come see the apartment I'm staying in. It's a loft on Mercer Street."

"A loft? In Soho?" I looked down at my black tank top and black jeans. "I don't think I'm wearing enough black."

He put his hands in his pockets and pulled up his pants until they came up to his shins. "Me either. But it's air-conditioned."

I looked at him standing there, with his sneakers sticking out like clown shoes, and at the expanse of calf revealed. I'd been too busy the other night to notice what nice ankles he had. "Okay," I said, still ogling at them. "I'll come."

"You will?" Ray looked at me as if I'd just agreed to jump off a cliff with him. He wrote the address down on a corner of the paper bag, tore it off, and handed it to me.

"You know," he said, "the only reason I came down to Washington for the convention was because I knew you were going to be there."

Then he bent to kiss me, and I kissed him back, on his neck, where his shoulder and his sweatshirt and the nylon strap of his bag all came together.

I could tell you a lot of things about that night.

I could tell you how hot it was out and how I took a taxi to the address he had given me and how, when I got to the building and the elevator door opened on the fourth floor, he was standing there, out in the hallway, waiting for me.

I could tell you what he wore and what I wore and what the apartment looked like, all three thousand square feet of it, with its huge windows and high ceilings and us tiptoeing through it, like trespassers, like two benevolent, misbegotten house thieves, whispering, snooping, looking without touching.

I could tell you how making love in a stranger's home, in a stranger's bed, with someone I hardly knew, felt both odd and surprisingly natural at the same time, the way wonderfully unfamiliar things often do, and how afterward, when he got up to put the cat out into the other room, he wrapped a long white towel around his waist even though no one else was there.

I could tell you how, when he returned with a cold bottle of water, he sat down beside me on the bed and we passed it back and forth, taking long, slow sips from the wet sweating bottle, and how good it tasted, and how we sat there for a long time, drinking and talking and listening to the sounds from the street, and how sometime after that, after I had removed the towel and after he had pushed back the sheet, how, a long time after that, when it was almost light, we finally fell asleep.

"So. Let's go over the facts," Joan said with intense, almost clinical interest after I told her everything early the next morning. Talking on the phone first thing in the morning from our desks was a kind of unspoken ritual—a way to debrief each other on our short time apart ("Did he call?" "Did you call?"); to restate unanswerable rhetorical questions ("What will become of me?" "What will become of us?"); and to plan the strategy for the day ahead based on what we had to work with from the night before.

"For starters, you work together."

"Correct," I said, taking a long suck off my Starbucks sip lid.

"And, he's engaged."

"Correct."

"Engaged. To be married," she repeated, pausing a second or two either for effect or to think. "Who is she?"

"She?"

"The fiancée."

"Oh. Mia. I don't know. I've never met her."

"Well, what does she do?"

I told her what Ray had told me.

Joan snorted. "I can just picture her. Walking down the aisle in Birkenstocks and an unbleached hemp smock."

I snorted. "Oh, and she's also a vegan."

"They've been together how long?"

"Long. Six years."

"Six years. And when's the wedding?"

"They haven't set a date."

"They haven't set a date?"

"Nope."

She paused again. "*Yet.*" Her tone was firm. Strategic. She must be good at this stuff, I thought, since she was secretly involved with someone she worked with—and someone who hadn't specified when—or whether—he and Joan would ever get married.

"That's good," she went on. "Very good. Considering."

"Considering what?"

She exhaled into the phone like I was an idiot. "Considering," she said as slowly as she could without not speaking at all, "that the man has already picked out *his wife.*"

"Oh. Right." What was I thinking?

What *was* I thinking? Maybe I was thinking that our two nights together were more than just a fluke.

Maybe I was wondering when he would get around to telling me that he was still in love with his fiancée, or that we shouldn't be doing this because we worked together.

Or maybe I wasn't thinking at all.

Joan lit a cigarette and blew into the phone. "Albeit that he's put her on layaway."

I lit a cigarette too. Strategy had never been my strong suit—the incomprehensible chess game, the ability to think three or four moves ahead and act accordingly (that is, defensively). At best I'd only been able to think one or two moves ahead. So I played with the phone cord and stared out the window, waiting for her to tell me what to do.

"Okay. This is what you do," she said. "You pretend she doesn't exist."

"What do you mean?"

"Never mention her. If he does, you nod politely, and then you change the subject."

"But why?"

"Look. You like him, right?"

"Right."

"And you'd like him to dump her, right?"

"Right."

"Well, if you *acknowledge* her existence—talk about her, ask about her—he'll never leave her. He'll know you want him to, and he'll start to feel pushed, and resentful. This way he'll think you could care less, and that will drive him crazy." She paused for a few seconds and then cackled at the obvious absurdity of what she'd just said. "I mean, I pretend that I could care less about Ben and look how well it's worked for me." Ben was the editor in chief of *Men's Times,* and she had been seeing him for almost two years, even though she frequently complained to me that she didn't know where their relationship was going.

"Listen," I said, getting a headache. "All I really wanted to know was what to do right now. When I see him. In the meeting. In five minutes."

"Oh." She sniffed. "That's easy. Pretend *he* doesn't exist."

"Really? Why?"

"Because men don't know how to deal with apathy and indifference. He'll be thrown into a tizzy, whatever the guy-version of a tizzy is."

We all met in the greenroom, taking our usual seats around the table like a family sitting down to Sunday dinner in some Diane Arbus photograph. When Ray walked in and sat down across from me, I felt so much adrenaline shoot through me that I thought I could almost see my hands shaking. Our eyes met and we both blushed instantly, then smiled, then looked away—Ray turning to Evelyn to share her copy of the agenda, and me turning to Eddie in desperation.

"Think she'll ask me again about Kevin Costner?" I whispered.

He turned and stared at me, and when he did, I noticed a rather large hickey on his neck. The size and shape of it shocked me, as did the fact that I thought I could almost make out teeth marks.

Eddie acknowledged my acknowledgment of his hickey by turning back to his legal pad and lighting a cigarette. "I bit myself shaving," he said, deadpan, then grinned slyly. Grinning seemed to make the hickey move slightly and change shape, like a tattoo on a flexed muscle, and I couldn't take my eyes off of it. I also couldn't help running the tip of my tongue over the edge of my two front teeth, trying to imagine what it was like to suck a piece of neck hard enough to cause internal bleeding.

Diane started talking about ratings and news stories, about who she wanted to book and who she didn't, and as she flipped through her papers and pointed up at the unusually empty schedule board, I felt Ray's knee touch mine.

"What do you think, Jane?" I heard Diane say.

What are the chances of your getting Ray every night this week?

I looked up at Ray, who was smiling and seemed guilty only of doodling on his pad, then at Diane, then at the empty board across the room, and as I flipped open my date book and uncapped my pen, I thought:

I think they're good, Diane. I think they're very good.

"Can I ask you something?"

Ray and I were sitting on a bench in Central Park after work. His arm was around me, and the sun was going down. "Are you seeing anyone, besides me?"

I looked up at him. For a second I considered lying, considered telling him that I was seeing several people, none of them seriously. It was the no-one-wants-to-eat-at-a-diner-where-there-are-no-cars-parked-in-front theory of why men shy away from women who aren't in demand—a theory which was tactfully passed on to me by a guy from Bay Ridge, Brooklyn, that I'd gone out with a few times several years before. But because I'd never lied about that and didn't think I'd be able to sound convincing, and because it somehow seemed unnecessary to lie to Ray at that moment, in that perfect fading light, under all those trees, I shook my head.

"No," I said. "I'm not seeing anyone. Besides you."

(What an idiot I was.

Always, *always* lie.)

Ray sighed heavily, and when he did, I felt his chest fall, and his arm pulled me closer to him. "I have to admit," he said, "I'm glad you're not seeing anyone."

"Are you?" I asked, somewhat disingenuously. Like a good lawyer, I'd learned from Joan, never ask a question like that without being ninety-nine percent sure of what the answer will be.

He stared at me. "Of course I am."

"So you're not secretly involved with Evelyn?"

"Evelyn? Why do you say that?"

"Because you spend a lot of time together in the office. And because you came down to Washington together."

He stretched his legs out in front of him. "No, Evelyn and I are just friends. Although I think sometimes she's wondered why there hasn't been more between us."

I stretched my legs out too and touched his foot with mine. "Why hasn't there been?"

"Because of Mia," he said. "And because she isn't really my type."

I looked at him. "Oh? And what is your type?"

He took my hand and squeezed it hard. "You." He smiled. "You're my type."

"Can I ask you something else?" I said. Darkness had fallen almost completely, and I looked up through the branches at what was left of the sky. Despite Joan's advice, I needed to know where things stood—where I stood—no matter how impossibly premature it was to form the question or trust the answer. And no matter how well I knew that asking was against the rules (read: *their* rules)—that it could tip your hand enough for the game to stop, I suddenly decided that I'd had enough of keeping myself in the dark until it was too late. So I asked.

"Have you told Mia anything about this? About—" I hesitated for a moment and decided not to use the word *us*.

Ray kicked at the gravel under his feet. "No. Not yet. I'm her only friend, really, and somehow I feel like she would be devastated if I abandoned her."

I paused, feeling another rush of New-Cow hormones coming on. "Are you going to tell her?"

He looked at me. "Of course," he said. "Of course I'm going to tell her. I have to."

I smiled, relieved. *New Cows always believe everything Bulls tell them.*

He stood up and I stood up and we started walking. It was almost nine o'clock and the park was silent, except for the sound of distant cars and the wind rustling through the tops of the trees. Ray put his arm around me and kissed my forehead.

"Let's go home," he said, and though I didn't know which home he was referring to, his or mine, I leaned against him and followed him out of the park and into a cab.

That night, when we were in bed, in my apartment, as it turned out, lying under the sheet, Ray said, "Tell me about your old boyfriends."

(It is only a matter of time before they ask you this.

Men are obsessed with this question, and they delude themselves—and you—with the idea that their interest in asking and your answering is purely clinical and informational: that is, that the details you disclose during warm, fuzzy moments like these will never come back to haunt you.)

So I refused.

"Why not?" Ray asked.

"Because."

"Because there are too many?"

"No. Because there were too few."

"Tell me about Michael, then."

"I already told you about him."

"Tell me more."

I turned away from Ray and stared at the wall. "Why?"

"Because," he said, pulling me back toward him, "I'm curious."

Curious George. My long-lost monkey crush.

I pulled the sheet up under my arms and looked at the ceiling. "There's not much more to tell," I lied. "We lived together for three years. We used to talk about getting married, but it didn't work out."

Ray rested his head on his hand and leaned his elbow into the pillow. Obviously he wasn't going anywhere. "Why not?"

"We argued a lot."

"About what?"

"About sex mostly."

Ray raised an eyebrow. "What about sex?"

I rolled my eyes and exhaled loudly. "About how we didn't do it enough."

Ray nudged me under the sheet. "I think we do it enough."

"You would, considering that 'doing it' hasn't exactly been the mainstay of your *other* relationship."

He laughed but wouldn't be distracted from the question at hand. "Go on," he said.

I closed my eyes and tried to think of a way to say the rest of it without really saying it, but because Ray was always telling me about how unhappy he was with Mia and because I felt somehow that if anyone would understand, he would, I finally just said this: "I think he wanted someone smarter."

Ray looked at me. *"Smarter?"*

I nodded.

"Than *you*?"

I shrugged, pretending it hadn't registered that he'd taken it for granted that I was smart. But it had registered. As sharply and as deeply as Michael's belief had that I wasn't.

"What was he, fucking chapter president of *Mensa*?"

I shrugged again.

"You mean, he came home one day and said, 'You're stupid.' "

"Not exactly." It hadn't just been one day, and it hadn't been expressed so eloquently.

Ray touched my hair, and we looked at each other for a minute or two without saying anything.

"Were you ever happy with him?"

I sighed. "I don't know. I thought I was. I remember being happy at the beginning and then a few flashes in the middle and at the end. I loved him and he loved me, and at the time I thought being in love and being happy was all the same thing. But I guess sometimes it isn't."

Ray moved on top of me and took my face in his hands. "Are you happy with me?"

I stared into his eyes, eyes that were kinder than any I had ever seen looking back at me. "Yes," I whispered. "I'm happy with you."

[MATING SCENE DELETED.]

POST-COPULATORY PHASE: STAGE II
THE BLISS OF MATING

When two people find each other attractive, their bodies quiver with a gush of PEA (phenylethylamine), a molecule that speeds up the flow of information between nerve cells. An amphetamine-like chemical, PEA whips the brain into a frenzy of excitement, which is why lovers feel euphoric, rejuvenated, optimistic, and energized, happy to sit up talking all night or making love for hours on end. Because "speed" is addictive, even the body's naturally made speed, some people become what Michael Liebowitz and Donald Klein of the New York State Psychiatric Institute refer to as "attraction junkies," needing a romantic relationship to feel excited by life.

—Diane Ackerman, *The Nature of Love*

·☾ ☽·

IT IS, OF COURSE, bliss to mate!

It is beyond description!

The ecstasy of it!

The rapture of it!

There are no words, really, or maybe, there are too many, and they've all been used already, so you should just shut up.

But you can't.

You won't.

You are a New Cow now, and the whole world must know about it!

You tell your friends, you tell acquaintances, you tell strangers—all of whom, you suspect with pity, have no idea what you're talking about since *they* have probably never *really* mated, not like *this,* anyway.

They look at you like you are mad, possessed, and you are: *You have New-Cow disease and it shows*—the inexcusable clichés, the ridiculous hyperbole, the disgusting earnestness, the incessant messianic need to enlighten the unenlightened:

You can't imagine . . . !

It's the most amazing . . . !

It's impossible to put into . . . !

If only you could hear yourself: your complete lack of irony, your complete lack of humor, your complete lack of wit, all those fucking ellipses . . . and *italics* and exclamation points!

But you can't. The sound of your own mooing is deafening.

———

And so we were happy.

Blissfully, ecstatically, elatedly, annoyingly, cloyingly happy.

During the ten days that followed we'd pass each other in the hallways or in the studio, trying not to let on that anything was going on between us since everyone knew about Ray's engagement status—one aspect of Ray that Joan didn't like much.

"Why is he keeping you such a secret?" she'd ask me, and I'd tell her that as soon as he told Mia, we wouldn't have to be so sneaky. Which made sense to me even if I didn't like being hidden and even if I didn't know exactly when he planned on telling her.

In the evenings he'd stop by my office, and we'd make a plan for how and when and where we would meet next. The nights he had to stay home with Mia I'd pace around the tight square of my apartment with the phone, listening to Joan script ultimatums, but on all the other nights we'd meet at my apartment, where he would always tell me, early in the morning when we'd first wake up, or late at night right before we'd fall asleep, that I made him feel things he'd never felt before.

"It's like a dream," he would say in a whisper.

And it was.

It was as close a place to heaven as I had ever imagined, and those first two weeks, as I walked through those gates and beheld the promise of the future, it seemed we would always exist there, forever suspended in the blissful, ecstatic, elated glow of each other's adoration.

POST-COPULATORY PHASE: STAGE III
THE EMERGENCE AND INTEGRATION
OF A NEW MALE INTO THE GROUP

The chances are that most of the females will agree with each other on which are the best males, since they all have the same information to go on.

—Richard Dawkins, *The Selfish Gene*

·☾ ☽·

I'D BEEN THINKING, as the days with Ray wore on, that the time had come for him to meet David and Joan and vice versa. It seemed a necessary step in all of my relationships—not only so Ray could know and understand me better by meeting my two closest friends but also, and perhaps more important, so David and Joan, my judge and jury, could provide an objective opinion about the person I was becoming increasingly involved with.

Or, at least, a semi-objective opinion.

Joan, I knew, would focus on all the practical aspects of whether or not Ray was worthy of me: Was he attractive? Articulate? Well mannered? Duly attentive and infatuated? A pivotal issue would be humor, about which she would declare at the end of the evening or the following morning one of two things: "Funny" or "Not funny."

David too would address all those points, but his opinion would ultimately come down to one immutable thing: the bullshit factor. Being "one of them" himself, he'd once explained to me, it was only natural that he could be a better judge of a man's character than I could: He knew the game and how it was played. David had a sixth sense about male falseness; could detect it in the most unobvious of circumstances and was rarely proven wrong.

And so I guess I should have paid attention when David asked me if I'd met any of Ray's friends yet, which I hadn't. But I was too preoccupied with Ray's meeting my friends. It wouldn't exactly be a carefree event for me since so much was at stake, but I looked forward to it. I was confident that Ray would pass their tests with flying colors.

And so, obviously, was he.

"I was wondering when you were going to bring me home to meet the family," he'd said when I asked him one night as we were leaving the office. It was one of the few nights we weren't going to spend together—he had to see Mia and I had bills to pay. Ray looked in his date book after we got off the elevator and told me the few nights that week that didn't work for him, and then we said good-bye—not kissing because we never kissed anywhere near the office.

Once I'd arranged the date—the following Thursday night—I told Ray.

"I'll even cook," he offered, and I readily agreed.

Ray in an apron would most certainly put him over the top.

But a week later, an hour before Joan and David were due to arrive at eight, Ray, who'd been holed up in my kitchen since the minute we'd come back to my apartment from work, cracked under the pressure.

"Maybe I should go home and change," he said, pulling at his white shirt.

"Why?" I said.

"I don't know. Maybe I should wear a tie. Or a different shirt. A blue shirt."

"You look perfect. You always look perfect."

"Are you sure?" He walked over to look at himself again in the full-length mirror on the inside of my closet door. "I want to make a good impression. I just—well, I really want them to like me."

I walked over to him and put my arms around his waist

from behind. "They will," I said. Then I went into the kitchen and swallowed two mouthfuls of bourbon.

"So what do you think they thought?" Ray asked me the minute they'd left, full of his poached salmon and the delight of having regaled him with stories about my epic fear of water bugs.

"I think they liked you," I said, making a trip to the kitchen with both hands full of dishes. Ray followed.

"Are you sure?"

"Of course I'm sure."

"But why?" He stood next to me at the sink, hovering obsessively.

"Why do I think they liked you, or why am I sure they did?"

"Both."

"Because," I said, hoping the word would answer both questions.

"No really," he said. "I mean, I barely said anything. I was just laughing like an asshole the whole night."

"Listen, obviously they liked you. I like you. You're immensely likable."

"But why?"

"You mean, besides the apron?"

He nodded.

I turned and stared at him. "Are you serious?"

"Kind of."

"Why is it so important whether they liked you or not? Or whether you liked them or not?"

"I liked them."

"But why do you care so much?"

He picked at a piece of the leftover apple tart but quickly grew bored with it. "Because I hate it when people don't like me. Mia's friends never liked me. I never knew what to say, and then when I'd think of something, it was never the right thing. Dinners were always like an E. F. Hutton commercial: Whenever I opened my mouth, they'd all stop talking and listen, as if they were sure I was going to say something politically offensive. Which I guess I did after a while. On purpose."

"But tonight wasn't like that. Joan loved you. I could tell. She would never have talked so much if she didn't like you." Which was true. Joan would have just sat there looking either extremely bored or extremely annoyed.

"And what about David?"

"What about David?"

"I don't know. I felt like he was watching me the whole time. As if he knew something I didn't."

"That's just the way he is. He's very protective of me. Like a brother would be if I had one. We've known each other a long time—he was there when I was with Michael, and I was there when he still slept with girls. We know a lot about each other that no one else knows, and we understand each other in ways other people don't. If he was watching you, he was doing it for me. To make sure I'm not going to get screwed."

"Is that what you're afraid of?"

"I'm always afraid of that."

Ray looked at me. "I'll never screw you," he said, pulling me out of the kitchen and over toward the bed. "At least not like that."

[SCREWING SCENE DELETED.]

"Funny," Joan declared first thing the next morning when she called me at the office. "Definitely funny."

"You think?"

"Hilarious."

"Really?" I tried to remember Ray being hilarious the night before, but nothing came immediately to mind, so I thought I'd just take the compliment and run.

"Also, very, very cute."

"I know."

"I'm sure you do. Great hands too."

"I know."

"Very important."

"The most important."

"Can't get very far without great hands."

"I know."

"And very attentive. You should see the way he looks at you. Turning his chair to stare at you while you're talking. Ben never does that. Look rapt."

"Wrapped?"

"Rapt. As in fascinated. Mesmerized. Enchanted. All of which Ray looked the entire evening."

"So . . . ?"

"So I approve. As soon as he ditches the phantom vegan . . ."

One down.

One to go.

I waited all morning to hear from David, but by noon he hadn't called, so I called him.

"So what'd you think?" I asked when I reached him at his studio.

"Great dinner," he said.

"And?" I said expectantly. "What did you think about Ray?"

"You mean, besides the fact that he has a great ass?"

I stopped short. "How could you tell he has great abs?"

"*Ass,*" David enunciated. "I said he has a great *ass*. Obviously your *second* choice."

I laughed quietly. "Third, actually."

"I see."

"But what did you *think* think?"

There was silence on the phone as he considered the question.

"David?"

"Yes, Jane?"

"What?"

David exhaled loudly, and I could tell he was fidgeting. "Look, he seemed nice. He seemed very nice."

"But?"

"But I don't know. I really don't know."

"Tell me what you aren't telling me."

He exhaled again. "I just got this feeling. This feeling like he was a little too good to be true. Perfect cook. Perfect looking. Perfect boyfriend. It's like there's something going on underneath all that perfectness, but I don't know what it is."

"Well, what do you *think* it is?"

"There's just something lost about him." He paused for a minute, thinking. "It's as if he's never really belonged anywhere. As if he's never quite figured out how not to feel lonely."

I nodded, as if I understood, but I didn't really. Not yet. I just waited expectantly on the other end of the phone for him to say something else.

"What?" he said. "You want me to tell you that you're going to live happily ever after? That your kids—all two point five of them—are going to be brown-eyed child-pornography under-wear models?"

I didn't answer.

"What do you think I am?" he said. "An *ass* reader?"

I thought all day about what David had said, but by the after-noon I had decided to put it aside, to chalk it up to the over-protectiveness I'd described to Ray the night before. In the past I'd always seen what David had seen, what he'd try to explain to me. But this time I didn't. When I looked at Ray, I believed what I saw:

Bull's bullshit factor: zero.

POST-COPULATORY PHASE: STAGE IV
THE VOCALIZATION OF EMOTIONS

With all great deceivers there is a noteworthy occurrence to which they owe their power. In the actual act of deception they are overcome by *belief in themselves:* it is this which then speaks so miraculously and compellingly to those who surround them. . . . Self-deception has to exist if a grand *effect* is to be produced.

—Friedrich Nietzsche
Human, All Too Human (1878)

·☾ ☽·

You'll never forget where you were when someone tells you they love you.

Where you were.

What you were doing.

What exactly they said when they said it.

Ray and I were putting fresh sheets on my bed. It was sometime after eleven o'clock on a Friday night, only two weeks after our relationship had begun, and we had just come upstairs from doing my laundry. The windows were open and it was raining outside, and I remember the smooth hissing sound the cars made as they drove by on the wet pavement.

I reached across my side of the bed to pull up the corner of the sheet and waited for Ray to pull up the other side. But he just looked at me and didn't move.

And that's when he said it.

He must have said something else just before it—something like *I've never felt this way with anyone* or *How did I ever live without you?* or some other combination of words that he had often strung together and that had always made him seem like such an emotion-filled person—but I don't remember exactly what he said. What I do remember is that he said it, and that he used my name when he said it.

I love you, Jane is what he said. And then, without really thinking, without really knowing if it was true, even though in retrospect, of course, it was, I said, *I love you too, Ray*. Just like he'd said it, just so he'd know how it felt to hear his name used in a sentence like that.

Ray came around to my side of the bed and said something

about fate, or about destiny, and I remember saying that I felt a very strong sense of some force too, of an invisible hand having led us both down separate paths to this point. And as we leaned against each other, waiting for the meaning of our words to sink in and settle, we both exhaled a long, slow, heavy breath, a breath that seemed to come not from our lungs but from a place much deeper and more unknown—the same place where relief comes from when finally it comes.

[MATING SCENE DELETED.]

In high school, when you start reading real books, about the suspension of disbelief—about how you will either be able to momentarily overlook a story's contrived details and petty inconsistences and fall headfirst into the hole of the narrative, or you won't.

Staring into a man's eyes, at some critical juncture of a relationship, trying to decide whether or not you will close your own and fall farther into the deep, dark abyss of love is much the same thing, I think. Though the latter requires more than just a leap of the imagination. It requires a leap of faith as well.

I used to think about that Friday night a lot, when I was still trying to fit the pieces of Ray's personality back together again. I used to think of him standing across the bed from me, telling me he was in love after only two weeks. Telling me he wanted us to move in together—without ever explaining what he planned on doing about Mia. And I often wondered what would have happened if I hadn't been sucked in by him that night, what would have happened if I had heeded the old proverb, "Why buy the cow when you can get the milk for free?" Or if I had, say, thrown the sheet over his head and tried to suffocate him, knowing that he would break my heart ten weeks later.

Would he have retracted it then and there?

Would I have been spared two and a half more months of bliss, and thus, given the calculations of the layaway payment plan for passion, two and a half years of pain?

Or would he simply have mistaken my horseplay for foreplay and thrown me down on the bed and covered me with the sheet too?

"He just came out and said it. Just like that. After only two weeks."

Joan and I had met the next day, on Saturday afternoon, at Aphrodite, a diner on Sixteenth Street which was halfway between her apartment in Chelsea and mine in the Village. She was staring at me while her hand went back and forth from the plate of french fries we were sharing to her mouth, and her eyes looked like they were open about a quarter of an inch too wide. Had I been paying attention, I would have noticed the split second or two between french fries, between sentences, when the expression in Joan's eyes changed from shock and amazement to sadness and probably jealousy—that thin curtain that comes down occasionally between two friends when one is happy about the other having something but wishes she herself had it too.

But I wasn't paying attention. I was too busy not eating, since "love" had made me lose my appetite. I fondled both newly protruding hipbones and sucked down another glass of water.

Joan finger-combed her hair behind her ears and stared expectantly at me again. "And then what did he say?"

I picked up one of her Marlboros and took my time lighting it, for effect. "He said he wanted to live together."

"*Live* together? Oh, my God. What did you say?"

What did I say? What *did* I say? "I don't really remember. I must have said yes, or something to that effect, because he left with the *Times'* real estate section."

She stared at me. "It took Ben almost a year to say the *L* word, and when he finally did, we were, you know, *doing it,* so it didn't even really *count*." Her hand pawed blindly at the plate in vain, since she had devoured the last french fry minutes ago. "I can't be*lieve* this."

I looked at the plate. "We can order more."

She stared at it and then at me, and in seconds her eyes narrowed into slits. "Oh, *I* see. You're trying to fatten me up while you get down to your *cohabitating* weight." She grabbed a passing waiter by his Naugahyde menus and ordered a piece of Boston cream pie.

"Eat," she said, handing me a fork. "Or I'll tell Ray what a pig you are in real life."

[DESSERT-SPLITTING SCENE DELETED.]

POST-COPULATORY PHASE: STAGE V
PREPARING FOR COHABITATION

A female, playing the domestic-bliss strategy, who simply looks the males over and tries to recognize qualities of fidelity in advance, lays herself open to deception. Any male who can pass himself off as a good loyal domestic type, but who in reality is concealing a strong tendency towards desertion and unfaithfulness, could have a great advantage. . . . [N]atural selection will tend to favour females who become good at seeing through such deception.

—Richard Dawkins, *The Selfish Gene*

·☾ ☽·

Fast forward:

Two months, ten days.

There was still this one little problem.

"So what should we do?" I asked one morning before work while we were still in bed in my apartment. *What should we do about the ball and chain?*

"We start seriously looking for an apartment is what we do."

Ray rolled over on top of me and kissed me with his eyes open. "Just think," he whispered, opening his eyes even wider with obvious delight, "we'll be able to do this all the time."

"You mean, not just when Mia's sleeping over at the shelter? Or away at some conference?" The latter of which was why we were together that morning. "Or when you tell her that you worked so late at the studio, you fell asleep on the couch in your office?" Despite his lies I couldn't help feeling flattered that he'd lied for *me*.

"No. We'll be together all the time. Every morning. Every night. Weekdays. Week nights. Weekends. The thought of it is almost too wonderful to imagine." He sighed heavily and paused for maximum effect. "My joy knows no bounds."

His joy knew no bounds?

How pretentious he sounded.

How affected.

But New Cows can't be bothered with the details of foppish language—they are far too busy enjoying their esteemed status and waving good-bye to their Bull's soon-to-be-ex Current Cow.

It wasn't the first time I'd noticed it, though—Ray's occasional lapses into pretentiousness. One night, shortly after we'd first met, when we were leaving the office together at the same time, we walked out onto the street and found that it was raining. I flipped open my umbrella and turned to look at him. Already drenched, he shrugged and rummaged through his bag.

"No umbrella," he had said, as he removed a thin-spined paperback book and put it over his head. Then he said a most revolting thing: "But e. e. cummings."

"I was thinking we should live downtown. Soho maybe. Or Little Italy," Ray continued, a beatific expression spreading across his face. "I've always wanted to live in Little Italy since I like to pretend I'm Italian. Except for the fact that there's no real supermarket below Houston, there's great shopping."

He rolled onto his back and ran his hands up and down his own abs, presumably checking to make sure they had not disappeared overnight. Reassured, he turned to me again and took both of my hands in his and kissed them. "I make a great sauce, *cara mia*. We'll find the perfect apartment with a great kitchen, and I'll cook spaghetti for you every night."

Despite myself and his annoying use of the Italian possessive I couldn't help being momentarily distracted by his pitch—even if one wasn't necessary at that point.

After all, I had been starring in the movie of my perfect New-Cow fantasy life for a while now, ever since he had said, practically in the same breath, that he loved me and wanted to move in with me. The only thing I couldn't quite manage to splice out of the endless reels of fantasy footage was the persistent plaintive mooing of that fucking . . .

"But what about . . . ?"

"What? Apartment hunting? We'll find one. A great one. I have a good feeling about this. And once we do, we'll each give one month's notice on our leases and be able to move in on September first."

The footage continued.

The bedroom.

The bed.

The sheets and pillowcases.

The kitchen.

The Calphalon.

The vats of marinara sauce boiling over on the . . .

"Actually, I was talking about . . . you know." I still couldn't say Mia without feeling a wave of nausea at the "uniqueness" of it. I would have been so much less jealous if she were just Susan or Donna or some other fat-girl name.

Ray released my hands and went back to fondling his abs, albeit more distractedly than he had before. He sighed heavily and shook his head against the pillow. "I guess I have to tell her, don't I?"

I rolled my eyes. "Well, I would *think* so. Unless, of course, you want us *all* to move in together."

The extra pillow.

The extra place setting.

The extra toothbrush.

The extra name on the mailbox.

All those macrobiotic cookbooks and packages of miso and fluffy clouds of tofu floating in watery . . .

"I know, I know," he said. "I know I have to do it. I just haven't known how. Somehow I feel like it's the ultimate act of betrayal, of desertion."

"That's because it *is*." I could hear myself saying the words slowly, *too slowly,* as if I were talking to a moron. "Look, I don't want to feel like I'm forcing you to do something you don't want to do. I mean, maybe it's too soon to do this.

Maybe you need some time between Mia and me to process everything. And maybe we shouldn't rush into living together just because in New York it's too expensive not to."

"I don't want to live with you because it's *cheaper,*" Ray said.

"I know." I paused. "It's just that if you really want us to move in together—to be together—then I think you better tell her before someone throws her a surprise bridal shower."

Ray stopped fondling mid-ab and looked stricken. "God. You're right."

"Not to mention," I added, since I had his attention, "the fact that it's wrong to continue deceiving her like this. I mean, if my fiancé wasn't in love with me anymore and was in love with someone else," I began, not knowing where I was going with that sentence but suspecting I was headed for a big, fat fucking lie, "I'd . . . well, I'd want to know."

"You would?"

"Of course I would." I clicked my tongue and hissed like a pissed-off twelve-year-old. "Wouldn't you?"

Ray looked pale. "I guess." He lay on the bed not moving, barely breathing. For a moment I almost felt sorry for him.

Maybe a triple bed wouldn't be so bad.

I put his hands on his stomach and moved them around slowly, hoping he'd catch on. But he didn't.

"You're right," he said. "I'll tell her. I'll tell her tomorrow after work."

The next night Ray didn't call. Imagining the worst about what they were doing (talking, crying, consoling, reconciling, having sex for the first time in however long they hadn't had it for), I paced, called Ray's apartment, called Joan, called Ray's apartment again, called Joan again, then swore to dump him before he had the chance to dump me.

But the next morning, when he walked into my office, he looked like he'd been hit by a bus.

"I feel like I've been hit by a bus," he said.

"You told her?"

"I told her."

"How bad was it?"

"It was bad."

I paused. "How bad?"

"Let's put it this way: We started talking at seven, and at four in the morning she was still crying."

"Four in the morning?"

Ray nodded. "I've never seen her so upset. It was gut wrenching."

Like I cared.

"I wish you'd come over afterward."

"Well, I couldn't exactly excuse myself. She wanted me to stay with her until she fell asleep, and I felt like it was the least I could do."

"You *stayed* until she *fell asleep*?" I hated women who made their boyfriends stay until they had fallen asleep on the nights they'd been broken up with. Besides practically forcing Ray into breaking up with his fiancée, it was the most pathetic thing I could ever imagine doing.

"I think so. I kind of fell asleep first."

"Really."

Ray sat down and took off his glasses, rubbing his eyes with his hands. "Look, I couldn't leave after that. We've been together for six years." He put his glasses back on. "Nothing happened, if that's what you're thinking."

I bit my thumbnail and stared at him. It didn't *look* like anything had happened—not that I was certain I'd be able to tell if it had. And besides, *nothing had happened for two and a half years,* he'd always told me. I stared at him for another few seconds to make sure he didn't take me for too easy a mark, and then I took my thumb out of my mouth.

Ray put his hands in his pockets and lifted his pants up above his ankles. "So. Want to go see a one bedroom on Mulberry Street during lunch?"

The twelve-hundred-dollar one bedroom on Mulberry Street had a pigeon nesting in the bedroom window.

The thirteen-hundred-and-fifty-dollar one bedroom on Spring Street had the requisite bathtub in the kitchen.

The fourteen-hundred-dollar one bedroom on Elizabeth Street reeked of kimchi and, though it didn't have a bathtub in the kitchen or a bird nesting in the bedroom, seemed to be architecturally deformed in some way I couldn't quite put my finger on. But after standing in the kitchen for a full five minutes, I squinted suspiciously at the refrigerator and the sink and the stove until it came to me.

"This kitchen has no counters," I whispered to Ray. He looked around and nodded. "It's not that there aren't *enough* counters. There aren't *any* counters." I stared in horror and fascination, as if I were looking at a face without a nose. "And it's not just that they forgot to put them in. There's no space for them."

Later, after we'd returned to the office, depressed and annoyed that we'd wasted our two-hour lunch on such a pathetic selection of apartments, Ray called me from the control room.

"I hate this," he said. "This city is a dump."

"I know."

"I mean, it shouldn't be so hard to find an apartment for under two thousand dollars that isn't a shithole."

"I know."

There was silence. I wondered if Ray's next statement was going to be that maybe we should quit looking for now, that there was really no reason to rush into a place we hated, that we should wait until we found something great and move then, so I held my breath. David was right, I realized. Of course it was all too good to be true.

"You know, I just remembered something," Ray said excitedly.

I just remembered that I don't really love you.

"I had drinks last week with a guy I used to work with at MacNeil/Lehrer. His old girlfriend, Tracy, who works at CBS, is being transferred next month to their London bureau. He said that she owns a co-op and either didn't have time to sell it or didn't want to sell it."

I exhaled as inaudibly as I could. "Where is it?"

"Chelsea." He paused. "Which is why I didn't really think about it then. I mean, it's not Little Italy, but at this point who the fuck cares, right?"

"Right."

"If I can arrange to see it, are you free during lunch tomorrow or right after work?"

I told him I was.

"Great. I'll call you back." And he hung up.

At the end of the day he called back. "Okay. Tomorrow after work. And it sounds amazing."

"Tell me."

"One bedroom. Brownstone building. Nineteenth Street just off Eighth Avenue."

"That's right near the Joyce Theater, isn't it?"

"Right behind it. She renovated the apartment about two years ago, just after she bought it. New kitchen. New bathroom. Refinished hardwood floors. Working fireplace."

"No way," I said. My fireplace was the one and only regret I had about giving up my apartment on Charles Street.

"Wait. There's more. Sunken living room."

"Shut *up*."

"I'm not kidding. I don't think it's like Park-Avenue-sunken-living-room sunken living room, but she said it's two or three little steps down."

"Sounds sunken to me." I sat back in my chair and tried to picture what the apartment looked like, and what it would look like with us in it—*the perfect Cow and Bull couple, the envy of all our friends*. I was so excited that I was afraid I was getting too excited. "What's the bad news?"

"The bad news is the money. Sixteen hundred dollars a month. That's her mortgage and maintenance. But it's a two-year official sublet, so once we're in, we're in."

"Fuck," I exhaled.

"I know. I thought in addition to the bliss of moving in together, we'd get the added-value-bonus bliss of saving money. But we can swing it." He paused. "So what do you think? You wanna see it?"

Of course I did.

From the moment we walked into that apartment the next evening we knew—or, at least, I knew—that we had found the perfect apartment. Standing there, in the little sunken living room, with the little bedroom and the little kitchen and the little bathroom all within view, I felt a thrill and a calmness I had never known before.

To borrow a phrase from Ray: My joy knew no bounds.

When Tracy left us alone for a while, Ray reached for my hand and walked us into the bedroom and over to the window. It was just after seven-thirty, but there was still light in the summer sky—a blue and orange and violet drape being pulled closed behind the rooftops of the city. He put his hand under my hair on the back of my neck and held my head against his chest, and I could hear his heart beating against the noise of the traffic from the street below.

"I love this place," he whispered.

I tightened my arms around his back and closed my eyes.

"Not just this apartment, but this place we're in right here, right now. This is how I always imagined it could be— dreamed it could be, this feeling of bliss, of complete certainty. But I never believed it would really happen to me."

"Me either," I said.

"We're going to come home here every night—come home to each other every night, after shitty days at work, and we're going to be happier than anyone else in the whole world." I lifted my head, and he kissed me on the forehead, then on the neck, and then he put his mouth against my ear. "I love you, Jane," he said, just like the first time.

And, as it turned out, for the last time.

POST-COPULATORY PHASE: STAGE VI
DIMINISHED BLISS, THE DAWNING OF
THE AGE OF DISCONTENT,
AND THE MYSTERIOUS METAMORPHOSIS
FROM NEW COW TO OLD COW

Despite the vigor of the male [animal's] courtship, he is actually in a state of some trepidation. In fact, in the early stages, when fear still outweighs ardor, he seems so insecure that any movement toward him by the female sends him fleeing.

—Mark Jerome Walters, *The Dance of Life*

·☽ ☾·

OF COURSE I didn't know that it would be the last time he'd say those words, that it would be the last time I'd be as completely happy as I was during those few final minutes we were alone together in Tracy's apartment.

But it was.

Later I would come to view that scene as the final peak in a series of peaks—the benchmark peak, the peak that would soon become the crest of the wave over which I would float, then fall all the way to the bottom of the ocean. Had I known that standing by the window would be the last good moment, the last true moment of my time with Ray, I would have done something to mark it: I would have told him that the breath of relief I'd exhaled the night he told me he loved me came from a well of loneliness and sadness so deep and so hidden and so constant that no one else before him had ever reached it, taken the edge off its pain. That his empathy and tenderness had unearthed it—my nameless, silent grief—and that was why I had felt so inexplicably connected to him.

Had I known, I would have gone over every moment we'd spent together—the nights in my apartment, in his apartment, in the apartment he had house-sat; the weekend we drove out to Sagaponack; the two weeks' vacation we took in August in Wellfleet, on Cape Cod; Labor Day weekend, when we stayed in the city and he bought me a pair of teeny-tiny gold hoop earrings and I bought him a long-sleeved striped T-shirt; all the conversations we'd had in the car, in the dark, on the phone, or right before we'd fall asleep. I would have tried, and undoubtedly failed, to express the inexpressible: that for the first time in my life I knew what it felt like not to feel alone; that he seemed to love me more than anyone else ever had; that I loved him more than I'd ever loved anyone.

But since I didn't know, I focused on everything we had to do in the coming two weeks.

Signing the new lease.

Breaking our current leases.

Figuring out what crucial items were missing from our combined dowries.

Packing, switching utilities on and off, arranging movers.

Not to mention the most odious task of all: Ray breaking the news to Mia that not only was their relationship, and thus engagement, really over but that he was moving in with someone else. That he was moving in with me.

And though I knew those two weeks would be bad—that Ray would feel guilty and miserable and that there wouldn't be anything I could do except ride it out and be waiting on the other end with open arms, matching pots and pans, and a new set of sheets—I didn't know they would be as bad as they were.

I didn't know a man in love could make himself disappear.

How exactly did Ray disappear? Slowly and subtly.

First came *I Can't*.

The *I-can't-go-to-Bloomingdale's-because-I-can't-possibly-think-about-buying-things-for-us-when-Mia-is-lying-in-a-puddle-of-her-own-drool-after-what-I've-done-to-her* excuse.

Then came *emotional exhaustion*.

The *maybe-it's-better-if-we-don't-see-each-other-tonight-because-I-don't-think-I'd-be-much-good-anyway* excuse.

Then came too much *work*.

The *it's-a-crucial-time-for-the-show-right-now-and-I'm-really-on-the-hotseat-to-make-it-take-off-and-take-off-big* excuse.

Finally came *witholding sex.*

The *yes-I-know-I-used-to-chase-you-around-the-bed-like-a-sex-maniac-as-recently-as-six-days-ago-but-I've-got-a-lot-on-my-mind-right-now-okay* excuse.

Well, maybe it wasn't so subtle.

Buried deep within the mysterious process of metamorphosis from New Cow to Old Cow lies a rhetorical question:

If you assume you're still a New Cow, but you're really an Old Cow and no one's bothered to tell you, are you still a New Cow?

Or an Old Cow in denial?

Or are you just a fool?

I never did figure out the answer to that question. Rhetorical questions lead to more rhetorical questions—circular existential chicken-and-egg questions, like Which came first, the Old Cow or the New Cow?—or discussions about semantics: differing definitions of words like *new* and *old* and *fool.*

But mostly they lead to more basic questions, like When? and How? and Why?

I don't know exactly when I became an Old Cow to Ray—at what exact moment he first pushed me through the looking glass and I stepped out the other side, transformed—though I suspect it was sometime right after we'd seen that apartment in Chelsea and right before we were supposed to sign the lease when Ray realized, suddenly, that he would be stuck with me.

Stuck with me. Those words can still make me cry sometimes, even now, and even though Ray never actually said them.

But I know that's what he was thinking then, and during

the weeks when he stopped calling. And I know there were probably other words he was thinking, too:

Saddled with.

Tied down to.

Trapped.

Those are words that come later, rushing in like antibodies, to fight off the old words:

In love with.

Live with.

Attached to.

Moo.

POST-COPULATORY PHASE: STAGE VII
UNCOUPLING

Freezing is a widespread response to predator alarm, but some prey species add a refinement to their freezing behavior. As soon as they sight a predator approaching, they swiftly dart around to the far side of a tree trunk before performing the rigid statue response.

If freezing fails to work, then the next step is to flee . . . [using] . . . an erratic zigzag course. . . . To be successful, the direction-shifts of the fleeing animal must be irregular so that the predator cannot anticipate either when or in which direction the next change of course will be.

Another technique is the dash-and-hide, dash-and-retreat method. This is employed by animals that cannot sustain a prolonged bout of fleeing. They make a sudden darting movement at the highest possible speed and then quickly freeze, staying quite still in the undergrowth. . . . They may keep this up time and time again, until, with luck, the predator finally gives up the chase.

—Desmond Morris, *Animalwatching*

·☾ ☽·

IF YOU ARE LUCKY, a man will dump you.

That is, he will take you somewhere, or call you on the phone, and tell you, straight out, in so many words, that it is over.

More often than not, though, he will not be so direct and you will not be so lucky.

More often than not, he will not bother to tell you.

He will, instead, freeze.

Or zigzag.

Or dash and hide.

Or he will simply disappear you.

Disappearing you means he will behave toward you *as if* he has told you that it is over, behave *as if* you have had the conversation in which he says, audibly, and to your face, that, for whatever reasons, he doesn't want to see you anymore and that he would prefer it if things could go back to the way they were before you became involved: in other words, that he would like to be friends now.

The problem with being disappeared is that you have *not had* this conversation yet.

You have *not been told yet* that this is what he is thinking, that this is what he has *decided*.

To have had this conversation would mean that the man you would have had it with would only be guilty of being an asshole.

Not also guilty of being a coward.

———

The countdown.

The drumbeat.

Three + x = *escape*.

At the three-month mark you can practically set your watch to it.

The only thing you won't be able to predict is which method of escape they will choose.

Three months, two days:

Ray had been avoiding me for the past two weeks.

Like the plague.

Like an Old Cow.

"What is it?" David asked when I showed up at his apartment unannounced on a chilly Sunday afternoon in late September. "Is Ray starting to give you the runaround?"

He said "runaround" as if it were some kind of dreaded but expected gift, his sympathetic tone implying that he was much more intimately acquainted with the bestower than I might be. He wasn't wrong. Ever since we'd moved to New York after college, he had indeed been with—and been left by—more men than I had.

"I don't know," I said. "It's like he's pulling away and there's nothing I can do about it. One minute he's consumed with self-loathing and misery at the thought of 'abandoning' Mia. The next minute he's consumed with self-loathing and misery at the thought of being stuck with her for the rest of his life. Then it's how busy and under pressure he suddenly is at work. Then it's—"

"What?"

"Nothing."

"Not sleeping with you?"

I stared at him. "How did you know that?"

He shrugged. "Because I know."

I paced around the kitchen and leaned up against the refrigerator door. I was terrified and I felt sick to my stomach. "Something's changed, but I don't know what it is or when it happened."

David walked toward me and sat on the counter next to the stove. "It's the tomato-seed phase. That's what men turn into when they get too *involved*—slippery, evasive, impossible to pin down—tomato seeds on a cutting board."

I stared at David. "But he's *in love* with me," I said. "He *said* so. Not to mention the fact that he broke off his engagement and we're about to sign a lease."

David shook his head. "I know what he *said*. I've probably heard the same thing, or said it myself, a hundred times. But fear is not a rational emotion. It changes people, makes them behave like animals—*caged* animals." He sounded weary, as tired of the collective fear of all the men who had left him in a panic of emotion as he was of his own. "It all comes down to the survival instinct: fight or flight. And in my experience most men, most of the time, pick flight."

Suddenly the strange sound of Ray's voice the last time we spoke on the phone the previous Friday night—distant, preoccupied, inexplicably uncomfortable—came back to me. We'd been trying to figure out a time to sign the papers with Tracy, and Ray used all the aforementioned excuses to explain why he couldn't, except the one about not sleeping with me, which he saved for the end of the conversation when I asked him if he wanted to come over. I felt even sicker now and looked at David. "So what do I do?"

David forced a smile, trying to signal that the situation wasn't as bad as it seemed. But neither of us was buying his body language. "I'm sorry," he said, momentarily distracted. "It just reminds me of what happened with Andrew, which I still haven't gotten over."

"I'm sorry," I whispered. "I guess I didn't know that." I stared at him and didn't say anything until he pulled me toward him on the counter. He put his hands on my shoulders and looked at me until I cracked.

"I *hate* this," I said, feeling the knot in my stomach tighten and my throat constrict and my eyes fill up with big hot tears. "I *really, really* hate this."

Three months, seven days:

After almost three weeks of Ray's not calling in the evenings and not coming over I was completely wrecked. I'd stopped eating, stopped sleeping, even stopped calling David and Joan. I didn't know what to tell them since I had no idea what was happening, and I knew if I called them I wouldn't be able to help feeling embarrassed and ashamed, as if I'd done something to scare Ray off or somehow exaggerated his feelings for me in the first place.

The Monday morning after my conversation with David, Ray stood in my office doorway holding a cup of coffee and bearing a faint resemblance to something I couldn't quite put my finger on.

And then it came to me.

Tomato seed.

"Good morning," the seed said, adhering to the wall with its hands in its pockets. It was smiling, but its voice was thin, as if it were greeting a fellow-colleague seed instead of the New-Cow seed it was supposedly in love with.

"Good morning," I said back, half-expecting it to move closer and kiss me once it made sure no one was looking, the way it used to do. But it didn't budge. It just looked at me and then down at its feet.

The seed was getting nervous.

It could tell that I could tell it was acting strangely.

It knew it had to do something to distract me from the truth.

So it slid.

"You look tired. What time did you finally leave here last night?"

"Late," I told it. Then I mentioned that I had tried to call it when I got home, but there was no answer. Checking its face and clothes for signs of fatigue and finding them, I decided not to mention that I had tried the studio too.

But it was too late. It slid again.

"Sorry." It yawned apologetically, taking its glasses off and rubbing its eyes. "I was in the edit room until after two in the morning trying to demumble the William F. Buckley inter-view." It tried to laugh but ended up yawning again—and slid-ing—instead. "But enough about me. How are you?"

I said I was fine.

That I'd been packing.

That I'd seen a couch I liked.

That we really had to sign the lease and start figuring out the details of the move since it was only two weeks away and since my apartment had already been rerented.

Then it really slid.

"God, this week is going to be terrible," it said, shifting from one leg to the other. "I'm completely swamped." It looked out into the hallway as if it had just heard Diane call its name, even though it hadn't. "Gotta go," it said, rolling its eyes. "*Mommy's* waiting."

I heard nothing more from Ray that day.

That night I went home and got into bed at eight-thirty with a box of Kleenex, sick to my stomach with confusion and panic. When hours had passed and there was still no call from Ray, I tried him at the studio, and after eight or nine rings he picked up, breathless and seemingly exhausted. I listened for a second or two before hanging up, the shameful criminal adrenaline pumping through my limbs. Maybe it *was* work that was making him behave so strangely all of a sudden. But the tightness in my stomach muscles and the silent sobbing told me otherwise. Though I didn't know why and though I couldn't quite believe it, I knew, the way you always know in that deep, dark place in yourself you never want to return to, that he was leaving me.

On the Friday before Columbus Day weekend I was going through my overflowing in box, getting ready to leave for nowhere, when Ray passed my office from the men's room and waved.

"I'll talk to you," he said over his shoulder, which, I later learned, was seed-speak for not saying "I'll call you."

Which he didn't.

But he hadn't lied either.

You see, he'd simply slid.

Are you still with me?

You'd better be, because here comes Eddie.

I continued to listlessly sift through the week's accumulation of junk mail and interoffice flotsam until I came across a notice that someone had apparently circulated in house about an available sublet. *Own room in spacious two-bedroom apartment. Cutting-edge neighborhood. Walking distance to great bars. Smok-*

ers only. There was no name, only an extension given, but I knew it had to be Eddie.

Cough. Cough.

I looked up and saw Eddie leaning in my doorway, looking like the Marlboro Man minus the Stetson and the swinging doors.

"I see you got my personal ad," he said.

Before I could say anything, he had sat down in my guest chair and put his booted feet up on my desk.

"Interested?"

POST-COPULATORY PHASE: STAGE VIII
FLIGHT, ESCAPE,
AND THE DEATH OF A NEW COW

As the middle of the country endured its sixth day of sweltering summer heat, operators of feed lots in Iowa faced a new problem—exploding cows. The extreme heat causes gases to rapidly expand in animals after they die of heat-related distress. In many cases, they literally burst. "We've got to get them picked up right away or otherwise when you pick them up all you get is pieces," said one Iowa resident.

Time

·☽ ☾·

"Eddie Alden—*the* Eddie Alden—asked you to move in with him?" Joan said when she called at the end of the day after Eddie's "proposal." "Is this a joke?"

"He needs a roommate, Joan. Or, actually, he needs money."

"Remember the Christmas party?" she said, referring to the one time she'd met him, which had obviously left a lasting impression. "Sitting there sipping a drink while some young drunken waif sucked on his thumb. I mean, he's attractive in a dissipated way, but he's kind of an—"

"Idiot?"

"Asshole, was what I was going to say. Who wants to live with that?"

I closed my eyes and tried hard to decide whether he was an asshole or not. I had never quite made up my mind about him; never quite known what to make of his completely anti-social behavior. But following that afternoon's brief conversation I thought maybe his aloofness was just a byproduct of depression. Or, given his excessive smoking—and skirt chasing, oxygen deprivation. But before I could finish hypothesizing, Joan jumped back in, thinking out loud.

"Now it's coming back to me. Something about an old girlfriend who broke his heart? They were living together and she moved out? Am I right?" Joan said, as if there were a prize involved if she was. There were few things she loved more in life than being right, and, luckily for her, she usually was. "Anyway, it doesn't matter since you're moving in with Ray."

I opened my eyes, then squeezed them shut again. "I guess so."

"What do you mean, you *guess* so?"

I leaned back in my desk chair and moaned into the phone.
"Jane?"

"What?"

"*Are* you moving in with Ray?"

"I don't know."

"What does *that* mean?"

"I don't know. I haven't exactly seen him lately."

"I see," she said, lighting a cigarette and blowing smoke
into the receiver. "Has he called you?"

"No."

"I see," she said again. "Have you figured out who he's been
sleeping with?"

"Who he's been sleeping with? What are you talking
about?" *What was she talking about?* "He's not sleeping with
someone else. He's not like that. And besides, he wouldn't
have had time to. He's been working until midnight for the last
few weeks." I lit a cigarette too and exhaled loudly. "Isn't that
why he hasn't had time to sleep with *me*?" I blurted.

"Listen to me," Joan said. "Rule Number One: There's no
such thing as a man who doesn't have time to fuck around.
They always have time for that. And Rule Number Two: If a
man isn't sleeping with you, he's not sleeping alone. He's
sleeping with someone else."

I rolled my eyes.

"Don't roll your eyes. It's true."

I could tell she was waiting for me to agree that she was
right again, but I wouldn't. Not this time. I had far too much
invested in my belief in Ray—in the belief that he was precisely the kind of man who would be sleeping alone if he
wasn't sleeping with me.

That's just the way New Cows are, all right?

"Okay, okay, I take it back. Maybe I'm wrong . . . for a change . . ." she said in a tone of contrition she used when she realized she'd gone too far and unintentionally hit a nerve. "Look, if I were you, I'd have a talk with Ray. Soon. This isn't normal."

"I know," I said. And I did.

"Just talk to him," she said, her voice softening. "Whatever he says, it can't be any worse than not knowing."

Oh, yes it can be.

"So . . ." I said when Ray and I met after work the Tuesday following the long weekend. The meeting was my idea; the hair bar in the East Village was his.

That's because men don't dump women in private.

They dump them in public.

Where there are other people around.

Where they can't make a scene.

Men do this because they are afraid.

Hell hath no fury like an Old Cow scorned.

"So," he said back.

Seeing that I was going to need a little inside joke to break the proverbial iceberg—a *remember-me-I'm-your-New-Cow* kind of joke, I reached my arm out across the table so that it hovered above his hand without touching it. And I almost retracted it when I saw my hand shaking from the extreme patheticness of the situation: my having had to *ask* him to see me. The only thing I could cling to was the fact that he'd chosen the hair bar—a place where we had some history, a place that held some sentimental value.

Ha.

"Fourteen inches, Diane," I finally said. "Think we can make an exception this one time?"

Ray tried to laugh but couldn't quite manage it. He moved his hand away to reach for his beer, and as he did, I watched the muscles in his face pull and bend into an incredibly strained smile, one I would later come to recognize as a "false smile" (*The New York Times,* March 12, 1994). But the true horror came when I noticed what was revealed in the split-second transition of his face from nonsmile to false smile: pity.

It was an expression I suddenly realized I had seen him make before over the last few weeks, only I hadn't recognized it then, hadn't recognized the subtle distinctions between it, say, and its first, second, and third cousins: detachment, distraction, and remoteness. How was I supposed to know? Until he had disappeared, there had been no ebbing of our physical passion for each other; no visible fault lines in our attraction that would have made his look make sense to me, which would have explained why I was suddenly feeling sick to my stomach.

I held my breath and then exhaled it in one long, slow push. "It seems like something's been wrong lately."

Ray nodded.

"*Is* something wrong?"

"I don't know," he said. He scratched at the label on the bottle of beer he was gripping. His knuckles were white. "I think maybe we should cool things for a while."

I watched him work the wet paper until the edge of the label curled up and revealed the glue underneath, and tried to focus on his words:

Cool things for a while.

I translated them out loud: "You mean, not see each other. For a while."

He nodded. He looked troubled, burdened. *This is hard for*

me too, his expression implied. "I know I'll probably regret this. But I just think it would be best."

I translated out loud again, thinking this time, though, that I must be wrong—that I'd been wrong for the past two weeks imagining the worst and that he would tell me so: "You want to end things."

"The sex part, anyway. I just don't think I could handle that right now."

I was unable to translate that. I felt the way foreigners must feel when they come up against an idiom wall.

"Why?" was all I could manage before my lower jaw went slack.

Ray looked at me blankly, inscrutably. "I don't know."

"What do you mean, you don't know? You must know. There must be something, some reason why. Just tell me what it is. I want to know. I *have* to know."

Ray shifted uncomfortably in his chair. "I don't know. I really don't know."

I sat back in my chair and searched his face, but I found nothing in it that was familiar. The realization terrified me. It defied reason, negated the rules of intimacy. I shook my head in utter confusion. "But I thought you *wanted* this," I said, immediately horrified by the naked pleading in my voice. "I thought we both felt the same way—lucky, incredibly lucky, like we'd found *the thing.*"

"I did. I mean, it's just that it all happened so fast. Things started to get too serious all of a sudden."

I leaned hard against the back of my chair. A million thoughts exploded in my head—not the least of which was that in two weeks I would have to move out of my apartment and would then have no place to live. Only I couldn't focus on anything except the immediate matter at hand. "But things were always serious with us. Right from the beginning. *You* were the one who said you wanted us to live together. *You* were the one who said 'I love you' first. *You* were the one who broke your engagement. Why did you say all that if you didn't mean it?"

Ray looked at his beer and then at me. "I *did* mean it. *At the time*. But just because you say you love someone doesn't mean you're *tied* to them."

I stared at him in shock.

"Look," he said quickly, trying to recover. "That didn't come out right. I don't know how to explain this. I don't even know what I'm trying to say."

"Well, that's a first." Tears welled up behind my eyes, but I forced them back. I would not cry here, in front of him. Again I searched his face, his eyes, his mouth for something to tell me who he was, who he had been for the past three months, but it was as if a pod had replaced him across the table, and I knew, suddenly, that it was true what people always say about never being able to know another person completely.

"All those things you said, all those things you said you felt," I said. "Was it all just horseshit? Because everything I said was the truth."

He looked at me with more emotion in his face than I had seen in weeks. "No," he said. "I swear, Jane. It was real." He took my hand in both of his and held it tightly. "I still love you," he whispered. "I still want us to be important to each other. To be friends." He bent his head and kissed my hand solemnly, reverentially. "I'll never forget you."

I looked down at our hands and then at him, not sure if he was actually crying or just trying to make it look like he was. And then two words flashed across my mind: *crocodile tears*.

"I have to go," I said.

I was crying now. He was still holding my hand, and I was still too shocked to withdraw it, so I stood up slowly, steadying myself with my other hand on the table until we both let go. I put my jacket on, picked up my bag, and looked around the bar one last time.

"How ironic," I hissed. "This is where we started out that first night. And this is where we end up. You couldn't have planned it better."

Ray looked wounded. "I didn't plan on this part happening."

"Oh, *right*." I stood there, unable to move, as if I were half-expecting him to take it all back. But he just put some money down on the table, walked with me to the door and put his arms around me there in the ugly little vestibule.

And though I knew better—knew that I shouldn't allow myself to accept his comfort, his consolation—when his arms tightened around me, I couldn't help leaning my head lightly against his shoulder out of habit until I realized that what he was offering me was not actual comfort but only the memory of it.

Short of death, I think, there are few things sadder in this life than watching someone walk away from you after they have left you, watching the distance between your two bodies expand until there is nothing but empty space, and silence.

Standing there on First Avenue watching Ray walk away from me, until he was lost in the crowd of foot traffic and there was nothing else for me to do but walk away too, I felt the air escape from my lungs in a long, slow rush. And then, because nature abhors a vacuum, I felt a deep, heavy weight move in and take its place, the deep, heavy weight that was my heart, and I thought:

You asshole. You fucking asshole.
(Of course I would have taken him back in a second.)

It's funny now to think about how different I was then, how I still believed in boyfriends coming back, eventually. If Ray left me today, I'm sure I would make a lot of bitter jokes or simply keep my mouth shut. Because I've learned that most of the time they don't come back, no matter how long you wait for them to. But at that point I hadn't been left yet, at least not that way—for seemingly no reason, while we were seemingly still in the throes of passion—and so I still thought there were ways to bring people back, will them back, like mediums calling spirits.

David was the only person I knew who had been left like that, and when I trudged across town to his apartment and stood in his doorway shaking and sobbing, he seemed to understand what had happened and what I was thinking and feeling more than I did.

"After Andrew," he said, "I forced myself to go out, to meet people, to date. But every time I did, every time I was out with someone or in bed with someone, I'd think, *But they're not him.* And they weren't. And you're going to think that for a while too, because they're not Ray either, and somehow you're going to have to believe that even though they're not Ray, there's going to be someone else someday who will make you just as happy as he did." He sat down next to me on the couch and sighed, as if he knew what I wanted to hear. "Maybe he'll come back. And maybe he won't. But nothing you do will affect that. You can wait for something that may never happen or you can start trying to get over him now."

His words had a sense of finality to them, of hard-won

realism, and after they'd hung in the air for a few seconds, I realized suddenly that my life would never be the same.

Of course it wouldn't be.

I had gone through the looking glass and entered a parallel universe.

I had become an Old Cow.

[WEEPING SCENE DELETED.]

THE BIRTH OF AN OLD COW: STAGE I
ANGER, RAGE, GRIEF, DENIAL,
AND THE MOVE TO A NEW BARN

Persons suffering from . . . grief . . . remain motionless
and passive, or may occasionally rock themselves to and
fro. The circulation becomes languid; the face pale; the
muscles flaccid; the eyelids droop; the head hangs on the
contracted chest; the lips, cheeks, and lower jaw all sink
downwards from their own weight. Hence all the features
are lengthened; and the face of a person who hears bad
news is said to fall. . . . . After prolonged suffering the eyes
become dull and lack expression, and are often slightly suf-
fused with tears. The eyebrows not rarely are rendered
oblique, which is due to their inner ends being raised.
This produces peculiarly-formed wrinkles on the forehead. . . .

But the most conspicuous result of the opposed con-
traction of the [eyebrow] muscles, is exhibited by the pecu-
liar furrows formed on the forehead. These muscles, when
thus in conjoint yet opposed action, may be called, for the
sake of brevity, the grief-muscles."

—Charles Darwin
The Expression of the Emotions in Man and Animals

·☾ ☽·

You NEVER SLEEP the night someone dumps you.

There is too much pain.

Too much confusion.

Too much wrestling with your New-Cow suit, trying to keep it on while it is trying to come off.

Probably you will sleep in your clothes, too afraid to remove them because then you'll be confronted with your naked body—*the body that was left for countless imperfections; the body that will remain untouched, celibate, unmated for the rest of your natural life.*

You might lie on top of the covers because it is easier that way. Or, if you do muster the will to pull them down and crawl under them, you will have to be very careful not to suffocate or strangle yourself with them, though you will desperately want to.

Whatever you do with the sheets, you will curl up in the fetal position with a handful of Kleenex. You will sob and weep and roll over to no avail, since comfort and peace will elude you.

The words *Why? Why? Why?* will play in your head like an endless tape. After a few hours the words might become altered slightly, to *Why me?* or even *What will become of me?* These are transformational rhetorical questions and you should not try to answer them; they are simply part of the metamorphosis from New back to Old, and you must endure them.

At around five or six in the morning you will drift off momentarily from sheer exhaustion into a light and very brief REM sleep, from which you will awaken in tears. You will stare intently into space with your mouth open, then roll over again and sob into your pillow, because what you just dreamed was that he had come back, and for those few surreal semiconscious moments before you opened your eyes, you thought it was true.

The morning after, I got up and stared into the closet. Somehow I had the presence of mind to know that I needed to pick my clothes carefully to face Ray, something dark and impenetrable, something that could not, in any way, resemble a bathrobe and slippers.

But since I didn't own a suit, I put together something that looked like one: a mourning suit—black jacket, black skirt, black tights—and after I showered and dressed, I went into the bathroom and shut the door.

I don't know how long I stayed in there, sitting on the toilet seat cover, weeping, but I do know that it must have been a long time, because when I finally stood up and looked in the mirror, I almost didn't recognize myself. Staring back at me from the mirror was not the New Cow I had come to know and love the past few months but something else entirely:

A big, fat, sad, pathetic Old Cow with Kleenex sticking out of her nose.

All my efforts to prepare myself for seeing Ray dissolved when I actually saw him, in the greenroom, getting coffee. Our greenroom, unlike most television greenrooms, actually was green, a color long ago believed to have a calming effect on actors. As I stood there waiting for it to take effect on my nervous system, I was determined not to let him see how devastated, panicked, and suddenly furious I was.

"Hi," he said.

"Hi," I said with my back to him, filling my cup.

"Are you okay?"

I threw the pot of coffee back onto the burner and turned around. "Don't I look okay?"

"You look like you hate my guts."

"I do hate your guts."

"This is really hard for me too, you know."

"Right," I said. "You look really *destroyed.*"

"I am." His tone was both indignant and wounded at the same time. "Look, I'm feeling really fragile today."

"*You're* feeling fragile?" I rolled my eyes and snorted, "*Please.* I'm the one who's going to be homeless in two weeks." I could not believe that I'd been stupid enough to have given up my apartment.

Just then Eddie appeared. He was wearing all black too, like Johnny Cash, and when he walked over to the coffee machine Ray cowered slightly, the way he always did when Eddie was around.

"So, Eddie," I began. "I was thinking about what you said the other day. About your needing a roommate." I glared at Ray. "Since the apartment I was *supposed* to move into just fell through and my current apartment has already been rented, I was wondering if the offer was still good."

Eddie nodded. Ray looked from him to me in disbelief. "You're moving in with him?"

I shrugged, feigning indifference. "Maybe." Then I turned back to Eddie. "Tell me about the apartment."

Eddie took a sip from his coffee and then stared into it, leaning his hip against the counter. "Like I said, it's big. It's cheap. It has two bedrooms, a big living room, an eat-in kitchen, and a bathtub—in the bathroom."

"It sounds great," I lied. "When can I see it?"

He shrugged. "You can see it tonight."

I stared at Ray until he turned pale and looked away. "Fabulous," I said again. "Everything's just *fab*ulous."

Eddie and I left work together that evening and got on the F train heading downtown. I watched longingly as one by one the trains pulled into stations that signified more desirable neighborhoods: Fourteenth Street . . . West Fourth . . . Broadway/Lafayette . . . Second Avenue . . . until at Essex and Delancey, Eddie announced, "This is us."

We emerged from the subway into a neighborhood that, on any given day, I would be afraid to walk through in broad daylight. Only now it wasn't broad daylight. It was nearly dark at six, and we hadn't even turned the clocks back yet.

"Is it safe here?" I asked.

He lit a cigarette. "Safer than it used to be. The junkie transvestite prostitutes pretty much keep to themselves."

I felt better.

He pointed to one of the many corner bodegas we had passed. "You can get great pickles here. One of the many advantages of the neighborhood."

Much better.

When we got to the corner of Stanton and Chrystie, Eddie stopped in front of a big old dirty stone mid-rise tenement with fluorescent lights coming from the long, stark hallway beyond the vestibule. He unlocked the door and held it open for me like an old-world gentleman.

"The manse," he said, smirking. We went inside.

Up two flights of old white tiled steps was Eddie's apartment, which I took to calling the Lair, and later, after I'd moved in and made it my home too, the Halfway House, a reference to our mutual, and seemingly unending, recovery from our breakups. Eddie led the way, through the barely secured front door, down the long hallway with the wall-length coat rack, past the eat-in kitchen, and into the living room with its peeling paint and its book-lined walls and window boxes of ivy. Eddie's bedroom and adjoining study lay behind a set of French doors, and as I looked around the living room again at the mission table and the green brocade Victorian sofa and *objets d'art* scattered around it was obvious that an eye was very much at work here, and I remarked on it.

"My father was an architect," Eddie said, lighting a Camel and looking rather pleased with himself. No doubt this was not the first time a woman had commented on the decor.

I turned around again to take in the room, and it was then that I noticed the hole in the wall. Hole in the wall, actually, was a gross understatement, because what I was looking at was less a hole in the way that a mouse hole was a hole than a huge doorway-sized yaw in the plaster wall that adjoined the living room with what I suddenly realized was to be my room.

I pointed at the hole. "What is that?" I asked.

Eddie flicked his ash into the ivy and waved his hand, as if I were imagining it. He told me that one night he had spontaneously gotten the urge to "renovate," that he had started to knock down the wall to make that and the living room one "huge room." "I've spent a lot of time in Wyoming, and I like big spaces," he said, as if that would help make sense of his behavior, and, in a strange way, it did. But because Eddie looked uncomfortable and because I still couldn't quite absorb the fact that I was actually considering moving in, I let the subject drop.

So I asked him something else instead. "Is there anything I should know about you?" *Like, the womanizing? And the tendency not to engage people in everyday conversation?* Except for sharing an apartment with David one summer during college and cohabitating with Michael, I'd never had a male roommate, so I thought I should know, up front, if there was anything I should know.

"Like what?" Eddie said.

I thought for a minute. "Do you bring women home?"

"Sometimes." Eddie waited for a reaction, but I didn't flinch. "Do you bring men home?" he asked me.

The question caught me off guard, and I felt momentarily undone, as if the tight little fistful of will I had mustered to talk myself through the day and what lay ahead had turned into a fistful of air. I was tired and terrified and sick to my stomach with misery, but there seemed no other choice than to try, at all costs, to maintain some level of composure. After all, I couldn't afford the luxury of gut-wrenching sadness when so much was at stake: namely, homelessness. I shoved my hands in my jacket pockets and looked away, trying to hide my shame. "Not anymore."

Eddie eyed me. "Break up?"

I nodded.

"Me too. Recently?"

I nodded again.

"Me too. Well, a year and a half ago. But it feels like only yesterday."

I looked at Eddie, then at the living room, then at the pile of plaster chunks on the floorboards in my room, and I wondered if I would still not be over Ray in a year and a half. But it was impossible to think about that, just as it was impossible to think about having to move in with someone I hardly knew and barely liked because I had nowhere else to go and couldn't face looking at apartments again—this time without Ray—while staying indefinitely with Joan or David. How could I have been so stupid as to get myself into this ridiculous situation?

So I told Eddie then that we would have to do something about the hole.

Eddie told me that he would take care of it, that he would put in French doors, that it would look "as good as new," and I believed him. So I told him I would move in.

Eddie never did put up any French doors, so we put up a curtain instead, an old white sheet that we nailed into what was left of the studs. I put almost everything I owned into temporary storage and moved in with only a few essentials: some books, my clothes, a computer, and the manila envelope full of all the poems and love letters Ray had written me and all the photographs we had taken that summer. I bought a futon without a frame and put it down on the floor beside an old sewing table I'd picked up at a junk shop on the Bowery. Behind the futon was a big mullioned window that looked out into an airless black alley.

I moved out of my Charles Street apartment and into Eddie's apartment on a Sunday, less than a week after I'd come to see it. That night Eddie got up on a chair and put a fresh light bulb in the overhead socket and gave me a green ginger-jar lamp that he said he never used, and within a few hours my Zen bedroom was complete. I kept the books on the windowsill and my clothes on the shallow shelves and rack in the closet.

But I kept the manila envelope on the floor next to my bed, where I could always reach it.

Later the manila envelope and all that it contained would become the file of evidence. But back then it was filled only with what was left of Ray, and at night, after I'd turned the big light off and the little lamp on, I would crawl onto the floor and into the futon bed and pour its contents out onto the blanket and obsess over them for hours.

Then I would shut the barn door and cry myself to sleep.

[WEEPING SCENES DELETED.]

FIRST DAYS AT BASE CAMP

We think of science as manipulation, experiment, and quantification, done by men dressed in white coats, twirling buttons and watching dials in laboratories. When we read about a woman who gives funny names to chimpanzees and then follows them into the bush, meticulously recording their every grunt and groom, we are reluctant to admit such activity into the big leagues. . . .

The laboratory technique of stripping away uniqueness and finding quantifiable least common denominators cannot capture the richness of real history. Nature is context and interaction—organisms in their natural environment. The individuality of chimps matters. . . . You must observe in nature. You cannot take a few random looks now and then. You must follow hour after hour, at all times and places, lest you miss those odd, distinctive (and often short) events that set a pattern and history for entire societies.

—Stephen Jay Gould, the introduction to the revised
edition of Jane Goodall's *In the Shadow of Man*

·☾ ☽·

I DIDN'T SEE MUCH of Eddie that first week, since I left for work in the morning about three hours before he did and he came home at night well after I'd fallen asleep. But the following Sunday night I saw a hand come through the curtain. It was Eddie's hand, and in it was a glass of Scotch.

"Morphine," the hand said, ice cubes tinkling against the glass. "For the pain."

Eddie seemed to know about that pain, seemed to know its ins and outs, its cycles, its resistance to resistance. I took the glass and considered drinking it in the privacy of my room, but since I didn't want to seem rude, I put a sweatshirt on over my nightgown and came out through the curtain and into the living room, where Eddie was sitting in the dark on the couch with a glass for himself.

This would be the first of many nights that we would meet out there after Eddie had come in late, looking sadly into his penultimate drink, both of us beyond the consolation of liquor and cigarettes and our shared tales of misery.

And it would be from living with Eddie that I would learn almost everything I knew about the ways of men.

But an education is a relative thing, I found out—as much about the teacher as it is about the student, as much too about the answers as the questions asked, which is why I've spent almost as much time unlearning what I learned from Eddie as I spent learning it in the first place.

"So you never did tell me what really happened to my wall." I looked into my drink. I'd never liked Scotch, but Eddie made me almost uncomfortable enough to gulp it down. Something about the way he looked at me—or didn't look at me—made me feel like I was the kind of woman he'd never think twice about: I wasn't tough enough, I wasn't downtown enough; I wasn't pretty enough or sexy enough.

Not that I would have been capable of being interested at that point anyway:

My heart still belonged to my Cow-heart breaker.

"It was right after she moved out. I started tearing it down one night with an ax, but I stopped because I had to carry the hunks of plaster down at night in garbage bags so the super wouldn't see me and think I was carrying out body parts." Eddie watched me take a large sip from my glass and try not to gag. "Are you scared of me now?" he asked.

"Should I be?"

"Maybe." He laughed, then shifted on the couch.

I asked him, "Was 'she' your old girlfriend?"

He nodded and tipped his head back to drain his glass, and then he stood up to get himself another drink. But somewhere between the living room and the kitchen he stopped, as if he'd suddenly realized he was drunk enough and wouldn't need any more to sleep.

"Morphine," he said, walking back past me toward his room. "For the pain of Rebecca."

The next night, when Eddie came home late, I was in my room pretending to read when he knocked on my wall. A little shower of plaster chunks fell to the floor.

"Let's go downstairs," he said through the curtain.

"What's downstairs?"

"Night Owls. One of the bars where Jack Abbott used to

drink after he wrote *In the Belly of the Beast,* before he killed that waiter."

We walked in just after midnight, past the jukebox and the television set and the plate-glass windows facing the street. We sat down at the bar, and the bartender nodded at Eddie, an obvious regular, and set him up with a Scotch. Then he looked at me. I shivered at the blasts of chilly October air coming through the door when it opened and closed.

"She'll have a Wild Turkey," Eddie said, "with ice."

I stared at him. "I usually order my own drink, you know."

"I know. But you need hard stuff now, and you have to learn how to drink it."

He picked up his glass and sipped off half an inch of Scotch. "The first time we broke up she came back in a week," he started without my asking him to. "But the second time she left that was it. I'm still waiting for her to come back."

"How did you meet?"

"Blind date. We were together for three years, and it was perfect. Well, it wasn't perfect. I was a monster sometimes."

"You cheated on her?"

"I never cheated on her. She was the only woman I was ever completely faithful to. Except once, but that didn't count because she had just moved out the first time."

"That was, what, a year and a half ago? And you're still sad?"

Eddie looked up at the ceiling with a knowing look on his face, the way he always would whenever he was about to impart a piece of hard-earned wisdom about "relationships." "Yes." He sighed heavily. "But it's a different kind of sadness now. You go through a lot of different stages, and each stage has a very particular and distinct kind of sadness."

I looked up at the television set and then out at the street. It was late now, and cold, and I was actually starting to long for my room.

"So that's my story, not that you've heard the last of it by any means," Eddie said. "Now what's yours?"

Mine? I didn't really have a story yet. Months would pass before I would become truly bitter and hatch the Old-Cow– New-Cow theory and all its ancillary theorems. So all I could do was lay out the bones of what had happened with Ray and hope that Eddie could make some sense of them:

"I fell in love with someone. Who I thought fell in love with me. We were going to move in together, were about to sign a lease, and then, all of a sudden, for seemingly no reason, he dumped me." I took a sip of bourbon, and the warmth of it moving like a lit fuse all the way to my stomach made me understand for the first time why serious drinkers drink.

"Did he say why?" Eddie drained his glass and signaled the bartender for a refill.

"He said he didn't know."

He nodded knowingly.

"What? Does that *mean* something?"

"It depends."

"On what?" I said insistently, my voice betraying a desperate need for explanation.

But he would only shrug. "He probably just got scared."

I put my drink down on the bar, and my rage escaped in a controlled whisper. "Of *what*?"

Eddie seemed surprised by my show of temper. "Of you."

"Oh, *fuck* you."

"Okay." He grinned at me, but I ignored him and stared back into my drink.

"So who is this guy, anyway? Do I know him?"

I looked up at the television. The eleven o'clock news was over, and a rerun of *Cheers* was starting. For a minute I thought I should be discreet and not tell Eddie since we all worked together, but when I saw Ted Danson skirt chasing, I was reminded that exactly two weeks ago Ray had dumped me a block away.

So I sang like a canary.

"You're kidding," Eddie said. "I always thought that Ray and Evelyn had a thing."

I told him that's what I had thought too, once, until Ray had explained that they'd always just been friends. "Besides," I added like an idiot, "he said she's not his type."

Eddie sucked intently on a Scotch-infused ice cube. "Any woman is a man's type."

"That's bullshit."

"I speak from experience."

I stared into my glass. "You know what, Eddie? Even though I wouldn't have thought it possible, I'm even sadder now than I was an hour ago. Or maybe, as you would say, it's just a *different kind* of sadness."

Eddie sucked the last ice cube in his glass and looked almost pleased with himself. Obviously, misery loved company.

"Well, now I'm stuck in that office, and I have to see him every day."

He thought a minute. "There's only one true prescription for a broken heart."

"Which is?"

"Get back on the horse."

"Meaning what?" I was not yet used to his Rancho Wyoming shorthand.

"Get a new boyfriend."

I shook my head and took a perfunctory sip of my drink. "I

don't think so. I don't think I'm ready yet. I mean, this just happened."

"It didn't *just* happen. It's been two weeks already." He looked dismissively at me and then up at the television set. "Do what you want, but it's worked for me. Dating has become my sport and my pastime."

"Well, women are different, *ob*viously. We need time to get over things."

"You can get over things a lot more quickly when you're back in the saddle," he said, reaching for his wallet. "It's all I do these days."

Fat lot of good it seemed to be doing Mr. Morphine.

The following Thursday night I left work and went to a book party at The Rainbow Room for Diane's best friend who was now an author. The book, a novel titled *Save the Last Dance for Me,* was stacked on the bar and displayed on the tables. Well-dressed and self-important media types floated by, en route to Diane's friend, who was standing in the center of the room, air kissing and pressing flesh.

I stood at the bar nervously nursing a glass of champagne, unsure of whether or not Ray would show up—half-hoping he would and half-hoping he wouldn't—when I spotted Evelyn. She had put her drink down on the bar and was starting to pull on her coat. I was so happy to see someone I knew that I almost hugged her.

"Hi," I said, practically tugging at her sleeve. My desperation was palpable.

She turned to me and smiled widely. *"Hi!"* she said, as if she hadn't seen me for three years even though we worked together every day. She was so incredibly sweet, and while I sometimes wondered what—if anything—went on behind those big green eyes, I was immensely grateful for her enthusiasm.

We nodded at each other and smiled. I had no idea of what to say. There was something completely overwhelming about such blatant sweetness. It rendered me stupid and made me feel like little devil horns were butting out of my scalp.

"So," I finally blurted with thick sarcasm, "*great* party."

Evelyn's eyes opened even wider with wonder. "I *know*. I wish I didn't have to leave, but I'm meeting someone and I'm really late."

My face fell, but hers didn't. She was beaming—luminous, almost. We said good-bye, and I stared into the crowd again.

A few minutes later Eddie appeared with a tall blonde on his arm. Gracefully losing her, he made his way over to me, stopping to greet and kiss many other beautiful women along the way. As I watched him crossing the room, I suddenly got it: Eddie really was a very handsome man. Thank God he wasn't my type.

"One Scotch and one champagne," Eddie said to the bartender.

I looked him up and down. He must have gone home and changed after work, because he was wearing a suit—a perfectly tailored gray flannel suit and exquisite silk tie—a far cry from his usual Johnny Cash wear.

He felt my stare but didn't look at me. "What?" he asked.

"Nothing."

"You like my suit." He turned toward me, leaning his back against the bar.

"Do I?"

He took a sip of his drink and a drag off his cigarette. "This is my favorite suit," he said, raising an eyebrow. "It's my lucky suit."

I turned to him. "*Lucky* suit?" Joan was right. He was an asshole.

He laughed a long, deep throaty laugh and elbowed me. "I'm just teasing you," he said. "It's my *only* suit."

I grinned and scanned the crowd. Okay, so he wasn't a total asshole. "So who's your date?"

"Pauline," he answered, seemingly unexcited.

"She's beautiful," I said. "Is it serious?"

"It's never serious."

I finished my glass of champagne. The bubbles floated up into my brain and made me feel suddenly calm. I looked at Eddie and then back at some of the women he'd kissed on his way in. "Who were all the others?"

Eddie dropped his cigarette on the floor and stepped on it, then turned his attention back to the room. He indicated the various women with a subtle point of his nose and talked into my ear.

"The redhead in the corner talking to her bald boyfriend is Diana. An actress. I saw her for about two weeks. Very wild but ultimately unfulfilling."

I nodded. "She looks like she's twelve."

"She's twenty-two."

"Like I said: twelve." I took a sip from Eddie's glass and handed it back to him. "Go on."

"The tall brunette with long, wavy hair. That's Giulia. The Victoria's Secret model. Looks great in a thong but surprisingly not very sexy."

"Sure."

"And Emily. The blonde near the ficus plant. Chapin School. Andover. Radcliffe. Smart. Beautiful. Great cook."

But?

"Too perfect."

"I see. You're kind of picky, don't you think?"

He considered the question. "I know what I want."

"And," I said, "what *do* you want?"

Eddie looked distractedly into the crowd, as if he had just seen someone he'd been waiting for.

He had.

I followed his pointing nose and saw a tall, shapely brunette. I awaited his comment. "That," he said. "I think I just saw my wife."

IN THE BELLY OF EDDIE'S BEAST: AN ALPHA MALE, HIS GROWING HAREM, AND THE CHIMPANZETTE WHO GOT AWAY

The number of women collected into harems is staggering by any standard. The emperor Bhuponder Singh had 332 women in his harem when he died, "all of [whom] were at the beck and call of the Maharaja. He could satisfy his sexual lust with any of them at any time of day or night." In India, estimates of harems of sixteenth-century kings ranged between four and twelve thousand occupants. In Imperial China, emperors around 771 B.C. kept one queen, three consorts or wives of the first rank, nine wives of the second rank, twenty-seven wives of the third rank, and eighty-one concubines. In Peru, an Inca lord kept a minimum of seven hundred women "for the service of his house and on whom to take his pleasure. . . ."

—David M. Buss, *The Evolution of Desire*

·☾ ☽·

THOUGH EDDIE BROUGHT HOME no wives those first few weeks I lived with him, he did bring home many women.

Many, many beautiful women whom I found waiting in the living room while Eddie changed for dinner, or heard giggling late at night as they tiptoed past my curtain on their way to his bedroom.

And there I'd be, the loser, sitting on the what-will-become-of-me couch with the remnants of my loser supper of beer and toast nearby, or lying in my what-will-become-of-me futon bed amid the scattered contents of the manila envelope, wondering how I'd sunk to this low, low point.

The answer was always the same:

Ray.

Ray. Ray. Ray.

I thought about him constantly. From the first second I opened my eyes in the morning to the last second before I closed them in the early evening, drunk and bloated with liquid and solid carbohydrates.

I loved him.

I hated him.

I could not get over him.

Probably because I saw him constantly—locking his bike up in front of the studio; walking up and down the hallway with his purposeful walk; in planning meetings in the greenroom when I would sit across the table from him and wonder what he was thinking, what he was feeling, if he was sleeping with anyone, whether he missed me or ever regretted his decision to dump me.

Hardly, judging from his ability to derive pleasure and excitement from his job, which I was completely unable to do.

"This is going to be *great*!" he'd say after a meeting or in the hallway just outside the studio. "Diane's agreed to do a whole hour on—"

Whatever.

It didn't matter.

I didn't care.

Just the fact that he was happy about something completely impersonal and unemotional was enough to send me back to my office with an urge to shoot myself in the head.

How could we be so different? How could he be so fine when I was so not fine?

I couldn't concentrate. I couldn't read. I couldn't even watch television. All I could do when I got home was gum my toast and listen to the country music station Eddie's receiver was tuned to and wallow in the singers' sad, sorry stories, which I liked to think were almost as sad and sorry as mine.

And try to make sense of my daily encounters with Ray. Like this one, sometime in mid-November, when he came into my office and took something out of his pocket:

"Here," he said.

I looked up from my computer and saw him put something rolled up in a napkin on my desk. "What's that?"

"It's for you."

I stared at the napkin suspiciously.

"I made it for you."

I took my glasses off and swiveled my chair toward it, then poked at it with a pencil a few times until the napkin fell open. Inside lay three slices of what appeared to be bread.

"You made this?" I said. I poked at the bread a few more times until he laughed.

"This weekend. You know, since I have no life, all I do on the weekends is dream of food and make it."

I stared at him. *No life.* I had no life either, and the last thing I could imagine was having an appetite and waiting for the weekend to come to try to sate it.

An appetite for *food,* that is.

"I've been baking bread a lot lately," he continued unprodded. "It's good. Therapeutic. Very Zen. You mix it up, let it rise, beat it down, let it rise again, beat it some more."

Kind of like what he did to me.

"And then an hour later you can eat it."

Imagining him in an apron in his kitchen covered in flour and beating a pile of dough to pass the hours of his supposed loneliness had a surprising effect on me:

It worked.

For an instant I felt a thick knot of sympathy and nostalgia growing in my stomach—*I have no life too! Why can't we be lonely together?*—and I smiled at him as he moved to the doorway of my office and backed out into the hallway.

But an hour later, when I passed Evelyn's cubicle and saw two slices of the same bread on her desk, I wanted to uncover the warm towel from his dough head and beat him senseless, let him rise, then beat him down again.

Or this one, a few weeks later, when he called me after getting home from a work party I didn't go to:

"It's me," he said, almost in a whisper. Eddie had handed me the phone through the curtain. "I hope I'm not calling too late."

"No," I said, trying to sound calm. "We're always up late."

There was silence, I knew, because of my use of the word *we,* and I relished it.

"Really," he said. "Doing what?"

"Just talking, mostly." His question and tone surprised me, as did my capacity to lie and mislead him with innuendo.

Another pause.

Mostly.

"I didn't think Eddie was the talking type."

"Well, outside the office he is. He has a very active social life, as you know, and he's always sort of falling in love with somebody."

Ray was silent. "Is he falling in love with you?"

This was easier than I'd thought. But at that point I didn't have the heart for the game—*New Old Cows are very sensitive to hurting others the way they themselves have been hurt*—and besides, I didn't want to make it seem like I was totally unavailable in case he wanted to, you know, come crawling back.

"With me?" I laughed a little for effect. "We're just friends."

Ray sighed then and made some joke about having heard that Eddie sometimes came home during lunch to watch reruns of *Bonanza,* but I lost track of what he was saying because I was still reeling from his apparent jealousy about Eddie and me.

"So does he?" Ray said.

"Does he what?"

"Does he come home at lunch to watch *Bonanza*?"

"I don't know." I'd heard the same story too, once, a long time ago, but forgotten about it since I'd moved in. It seemed like just the kind of rumor Eddie would start about himself to make people think he was more disconnected from his job than he already was so they'd leave him alone to concentrate on scheduling his Victoria's Secret models.

"Anyway," Ray said. "I was calling because I went to that party tonight and I was hoping I would see you there."

I lit a cigarette and exhaled the smoke away from the receiver. "I wasn't really in the mood for a party."

Another lie and misleading innuendo.

I wasn't really in the mood to go on living.

"Neither was I. But Diane thought we should at least make an appearance—now that we're national, she said we have to see and be seen so she made me and Evelyn go."

"Schmooze."

"Booze."

Ray told me about the party, and then he told me how he'd wished I'd been there so we could have stood in a corner and made fun of people. Then, after a long, expectant lull, he said: "So listen—we should have dinner sometime. Maybe sometime this week. I feel like I never see you. I feel like—well, I miss you."

My heart pounded. "Me too," I said.

"And maybe I could see your apartment. Make sure you're okay."

"I'm okay," I said, which was only half a lie.

Things were looking up now that I might have a reason to put on my hat and little dress again.

But Ray and I never did go to dinner, and he never did come by the apartment to check on my well-being. Which, besides pissing me off, hurting my feelings, and depressing me, surprised me. But not David.

"Mind-fuck," he pronounced when I called him from the office one night, well into the second week of waiting for Ray to stop in and ask me to dinner.

Joan agreed, in essence, though she didn't use that term, when I stopped by her apartment on my way home.

"He's fucking with you," she said, gulping from a bottle of

water. She had just come home from the gym and was still in her black one-piece Lycra space suit. "Look at me," she said, wiping her mouth when she came up from the water bottle for air. "I'm sweating like a pig."

She poured me a glass of water from a different bottle and walked me out of the kitchen and into the living room. "That's what Ben does," she said when we sat down on the couch. "Whenever he's being an asshole—which is, like, all the time—but particularly when he starts saying things that imply he's feeling trapped or hemmed in, I try to make him jealous. I won't call when I get home from work and I won't answer the phone when I know it's him. Or I'll tell him I had dinner with some freelance writer guy, only I won't tell him that he was really ugly."

"So it works."

Joan shifted on the couch and kicked off her big white high-top cross-trainers. "It works. For about a minute. He calls and calls. Gets very attentive. Stops complaining about how he sees too much of me and starts complaining about how he doesn't see enough of me. Then a few weeks later, or maybe a month later, it goes back to the way it was, and the whole cycle starts again."

I shook my head. "What *is* that?" I asked, annoyed. "I mean, why would Ray call and say he missed me and that he wanted to have dinner and then not do anything?"

She lifted her hair off her neck for a few seconds, then reached for a cigarette and lit it. "I don't know," she said finally. "It's what they do."

"But why? *Why?*"

"It's like, they want what they can't have, and as soon as they can have it, they don't want it anymore. It's completely demoralizing to feel like you're reduced to just being some emotional trigger that sets them off. Like, it almost doesn't matter what you do or don't do. You're just a pawn, in this perpetual game of chess. And by the end you're so exhausted you almost hope you don't catch them." She yawned and ran her hands over her face and then down her neck in long, slow strokes. "God," she whispered. "I feel so *old*."

One night, on one of the rare occasions that Eddie was home, I made a list of all the girlfriends he'd had since I'd moved in. After I typed it up, I came through the curtain and stood in the doorway of Eddie's room, where he was lying in bed, reading *American Psycho*.

"I think I have them all," I said, as if I were the first one back from a scavenger hunt. "Holly. Diana. Tina. Bettina. Pauline. Giulia. Deborah. Emily. Melissa. Alissa. Elaine."

Eddie looked up from his book. He took off his reading glasses and tightened the belt of his ripped and threadbare Black-Watch-plaid wool bathrobe.

"You missed Jacqueline."

"Jacqueline?" I said, checking my notes. "Who's Jacqueline?"

"Between Diana and Tina and during Bettina," he started to explain, but it was taking too much effort, and he soon became bored, so he put his glasses on and returned to his book.

I dragged the phone into my room through the curtain and called Joan.

"There's so many of them I can't keep track," I whispered into the receiver. "It's *amaz*ing. It's horrible." The mere thought of them made me envision a conga line of bunnies, dancing their way through the Playboy Mansion on their way to Hugh Hefner's silk pajamas.

Joan was unimpressed. "Really," she said. "He dates *that* much?"

"Every week there's someone new. And these women—they're *gorgeous*. Unbelievable. Sometimes—usually—he has several different women at the same time."

"At the same time? In the apartment?" She sounded momentarily intrigued.

"No. I mean, he dates them simultaneously."

But no matter how many women Eddie could have, he always came back to the one he couldn't have.

"Jane. Wake up. I need to talk to you."

Eddie's silhouette showed through the curtain, and for an instant I was tempted to feign sleep and take one night off from his drunken rantings. But there was something in his voice that night which made me reconsider, so I sat up in bed and opened the curtain.

In the dark I saw Eddie pour himself a drink, and when he put the bottle down, he turned around and peered in at me. Then he shook his head.

"No. You're going to have to come out for this one. It's important."

I crawled out past the sheet, past the plaster chunks, and over to the couch next to Eddie. He looked exhausted and slightly drunk, yet when I looked in his eyes, I saw an unfamiliar spark of alertness. "What is it?"

"I saw her."

"You saw who?"

"Rebecca. I saw Rebecca. At the Film Forum."

"Did she see you?"

"Yes, she saw me," he said, taking a quick sip of Scotch and then a long, slow drag of his cigarette. "We sat together."

I reached for his glass and took a sip too.

"I knew she would be there. I went to the theater after work, and I just had this feeling I'd see her there."

"And you did."

"And I did. And it was great, of course, just like I'd always imagined it would be."

"So what happened?"

"We sat together. We talked. Afterward we had dinner." Eddie sighed and looked at his drink. "It was . . . perfect."

For a minute or two we didn't speak. This was the first time either of us had had a sign of hope, and we were too afraid to acknowledge it.

"Will you see her again?" I asked.

"I don't know." Eddie lit another cigarette and inhaled so deeply I was afraid the smoke would never come out of his lungs. "Maybe."

"Does she have a boyfriend?"

"Sort of. I think. She said she's been seeing someone, but it's not working out."

"Too bad," I said, and we both laughed quietly.

Eddie put his glass down and ran his hands through his hair. "You know, since she left, I've probably been with a dozen women—" He looked at my raised eyebrow and recalculated accordingly. "Okay, *three* dozen women—beautiful women, intelligent women, *rich* women. But when I'm with Rebecca, there's just this thing, this feeling, like I've come home after being away for a long time."

I took another sip of Eddie's Scotch and thought of Ray. "I know," I said.

"I'm still in love with her," he whispered, expecting me to be surprised. But I wasn't. Of course I wasn't.

"Do you have a picture of her?" I watched his face while he didn't answer, but it betrayed nothing. "It would help me understand everything if I knew what she looked like."

"There is only one picture," he said finally. "A Polaroid. And I had to hide it."

Eddie got up, and I followed him, not into his bedroom but into the kitchen, to the big, deep cabinet above the refrigerator. Standing on a chair, he pulled out a huge old cardboard box, full of hammers and nails and electrical wire and camping supplies, and as he passed me a saw to hold, he slipped something into the palm of his hand and jumped down off the chair.

"It was New Year's Day," he said, standing next to me under the light. "Two years ago. We had some people over." I looked into his hand, and there they were, in the kitchen by the sink, smiling. Eddie hugging Rebecca from behind.

For a moment I couldn't speak. Maybe it was because Rebecca was so unlike all the women Eddie had brought home those two months—a grown-up tomboy with regular hair and a denim shirt and no makeup—that I was caught off guard. Or maybe it was seeing the Halfway House in its previous incarnation, a place where two people in love lived together. Or maybe it was how different Eddie looked—how full of color his face was, how full of life his eyes were compared to now.

Eddie asked me, "Is she what you expected?"

I shook my head slowly. "I don't know what I expected. I wouldn't have thought she was your type."

His eyes were still fixed to the photograph. "She's exactly my type."

"She looks so . . . normal." I looked up at Eddie. "And you look so happy."

"I was happy."

I was stunned. Not only by the fact that Rebecca looked like someone I would probably be friends with but also because, for the first time since I'd known Eddie—for the first time since I'd moved in, he seemed almost—friendly. Like someone I could actually be interested in. . . . I stared at him for a few seconds and then felt a shiver snake through my body.

What was I thinking?

Shame on me for taking pity on an Old Bull.

Eddie stood there for a while, looking lost, but then he took a deep breath and stole one last private look at the photo.

"My Rebecca," he said sadly. He got up on the chair, put the Polaroid in the box, and pushed the box as far back as it would go, then slammed the cabinet doors shut.

"Back you go," he said to the woman in the picture, the woman who used to live here but didn't anymore. "That's what you get for leaving me."

A few dinners later, when Eddie came home the night he asked Rebecca if she wanted to get back together, I knew it was over even before he told me, knew from the way I heard him sit down on the couch without turning on the light or pouring himself a drink. And because I knew, I did not wait for him to ask me to come out.

There was no frenetic pacing this time, no strategizing, no lectured theories about time, and change, and second chances. It was as if Eddie had seen, in a flash of dreaded truth, that the black-velvet box of hope he had carried around all those months had been empty all along:

She was never coming back.

Looking at his silhouette in the dark, listening to his voice tremble and crack, I saw the dark tunnel of Eddie's loneliness;

knew that the women who came and went from his life only passed by it, without entering. And as I watched Eddie get up from the couch and walk into his room, I thought how full of tunnels the world was, each containing a different person, each with his or her own sadness.

"What about *our* tunnels?" Joan said the next day on the phone. "I mean, the man has hot and cold running underwear models and you feel sorry for him."

"I don't feel sorry for him. I just think he's interesting."

"What's so interesting? He's an animal. He preys on unsuspecting prepubescent girls and rips their hearts out. You're the one who sees the carnage."

Yes, I had seen it. And each of his hunt-and-kills was worthy of its own PBS science documentary.

But wasn't it interesting how, at times, he seemed almost . . . *human*.

EDDIE AND JANE
SEARCH FOR MATES

The female chooses not the male which is most attractive to her but the one which is the least distasteful.

—Charles Darwin
The Descent of Man and Selection in Relation to Sex (1871)

·☽☾·

AND SO THE NEXT few months passed. The dreaded holidays came, during which Eddie went to Wyoming and I went to Tortola with David, who was going to stay on there after New Year's for a shoot. It was a short, quiet vacation, and I spent most of my time lying on my what-will-become-of-me chaise watching David swim back and forth across the patch of ocean our private beach looked out on.

The first night Eddie and I were home together from our trips, we went downstairs to Night Owls for a reunion. He told me that while he'd been away, he'd made two big decisions: that he had to get over Rebecca once and for all, and that I had to do the same with Ray.

"I need to find a wife, and you need to find a husband," he said.

I sucked on some bourbon-soaked ice. But he was right, I knew. I just didn't want to admit it, and I certainly didn't want to start going out on blind dates, which is the route he suggested I take to accomplish his mandate. In fact, he said, he had several possibilities for me, including one guy he'd met at a wedding the previous summer, and two guys who came highly recommended by recent or current girlfriends of his.

Losers, I snorted.

But after another bourbon I agreed. "Fine. Set me up," I said to Eddie, which of course, the bartender took as a request for another round, which we sucked down without complaint.

"Since you're being so agreeable," Eddie said as we left the bar and stumbled back upstairs, "Giulia asked me if I would mind taking her cat for a month while she's in Rome for a catalog shoot."

I nodded drunkenly. "Sure. Fine. Whatever." I couldn't care less. "What's its name?" I asked him as he unlocked the door to the apartment and pushed it open.

"Evelyn," he said.

"Evelyn," I slurred as I wove down the hallway to my bedroom. "Evelyn with the big sweet face."

After each of the blind dates that Eddie had pimped for me Joan and I had virtually the same conversation:

"How was it?"

"Awful."

"Bad?"

"Jesus."

"So there was no—?"

"Chemistry? None."

"You're sure?"

"Positive."

"Not even—?"

"No way."

"Was he—?"

"Unappealing? Completely."

"Was there anything—?"

"Remotely attractive? No. He had that—"

"Thing?"

"With his lips. You know. Too—"

"Moist?"

"With little bits of spit—"

"In the corners?"

"In the middle. Like a little white thread."

"What about—?"

"His shoes? Hideous."

"Jazz shoes?"

"Crepe soles."

"Were you—?"

"Repulsed? Yes."

"What about his—?"

"Hands? Fleshy. No knuckles. Little."

"So you couldn't imagine—?"

"Them on me?"

"Or in you?"

"Never. No way."

"So if he called, you wouldn't—?"

"No."

"Not even just in case he—?"

"Has a friend? No."

"Did he—?"

"Pay? No."

"Did it—?"

"Depress me and remind me even more how much I miss Ray even though it was supposed to do the exact opposite? Yes."

"Well, maybe next time you'll—"

"There won't be a next time."

But there always was a next time.

"So what was the physical-feature caveat this time?"

"Big hair."

"As big as—?"

"Ours? Bigger."

"Jesus."

"Muammar Qaddafi hair."

"Oh, my God. Could you—?"

"See it from the street through the plate-glass windows of the restaurant? Yes."

"Did you try to—?"

"Block it out by putting my hands up and closing one eye while I talked to him? Yes."

"What would he look like if he—?"

"Were bald? Like Muammar Qaddafi with a stocking over his head."

"Wasn't he also the guy who—?"

"Just got off the Optifast program? Depends what you mean by *just*."

"Was he—?"

"Still fat or fat again? Yes."

"Did he—?"

"Eat anything? You mean, besides the two bowls of chips and salsa, five chicken-and-cheese enchilladas, and a chimichanga? No."

"Did he—?"

"Pay? Yes. For his 'half.' "

And a next time.

"Now, didn't you see this guy's head shot before to ensure against—?"

"Big hair and fat? Yes. But I should have known that an actor with a head shot would want to make—"

"An entrance?"

"A scene."

"Was he—?"

"Standing at the crowded bar with a huge hand-painted sign with fourth-grade-esque glued-on glitter that read *I'm your Mystery Date*? Yes."

"Oh, my God."

"And was there a big white beribboned box on the bar next to the sign that contained a big white beribboned wrist cour-sage? Yes."

"Jesus. Did you—?"

"Put it on because he said he wouldn't stop singing until I did? Yes."

"Were you—"

"So mortified that I had to run into the bathroom and breathe into a paper bag to control my panic attack? Yes."

"And was he—?"

"Still there when I came back, pulling file cards from his breast pocket with suggestions of what we could do on our *mystery date*? Yes."

"Did you—?"

"Want to kill him as much as I wanted to kill Eddie? Al-most."

THE QUEST FOR ANSWERS
AND THE METAMORPHOSIS OF
JANE GOODALL, OLD COW, INTO
JANE GOODALL, MONKEY SCIENTIST

Jane Goodall's first encounter with chimpanzees came at age two, when she was given Jubilee, a stuffed toy. Fascinated by animals, Jane later read Dr. Doolittle and dreamed of living in Africa. In 1957, at the age of 23, she traveled to Kenya and met paleontologist Louis S. B. Leakey, who stunned everyone by assigning her to study chimpanzees in what is now Tanzania's Gombe National Park. Her patient, unobtrusive approach brought her close to the chimps.

National Geographic, December 1995

·☾ ☽·

IT WAS LATE JANUARY, and Eddie had been going out a lot lately. As he reasoned, he wasn't getting any younger.

But his dates were.

Underage victim du jour?

A twenty-one-year-old Barnard senior.

"Why?" I asked him one Saturday night after he had put his lucky suit on. It was too broad and, perhaps, too stupid a question to ask, but I was annoyed by his never-ending supply of distraction while I had none, so I asked anyway. I'd been fairly subtle up until now with my questions about his sex life, but suddenly I felt like getting in his face.

Maybe that was because after almost three months of apartment sharing I felt I could get away with it without his really noticing—so sexless and uninteresting a fixture had I become in my misery and in comparison to his dates. Or maybe it was precisely because I had fallen so willingly into that role—into invisibility—that I suddenly wanted to break out of it, suddenly wanted Eddie to know that I was paying attention, that I noticed his incessant libidinous prowlings.

That I was a conscious, razor-sharp Old Cow who couldn't be fooled again.

Okay. So the real reason was that I was sick and tired of sitting home alone with Evelyn the cat.

"Why not?" he responded.

"What could you possibly have in common with someone fourteen years your junior?"

"It's not about what I see in her. It's about what she sees in me," Eddie clarified.

I nodded. "And what's that?" I asked.

"Everything."

Everything.

What an unbelievably huge ego.

The word resonated.

After he left I paced around the living room and then went to the dictionary.

Ego.

Egocentric.

Egoistic: being centered in or preoccupied with oneself and the gratification of one's own desires. See: narcissistic personality.

I flipped to the *N*'s.

Narcissistic personality: a personality disorder characterized by extreme self-centeredness and self-absorption, excessive need for attention and admiration, and disturbed interpersonal relationships.

Next stop: Eddie's room. The bed was neatly made; shirts and pants and dirty laundry were nowhere to be found, which was always the way he left his room when he went out on a Saturday night—to make a good impression on whomever he might bring home. I turned toward his bookshelves. Big dusty hardcovers and beat up paperbacks, some obviously left over from college and graduate school since they still had yellow and black USED stickers across their spines.

American history.

World history.

Nineteenth- and twentieth-century literature.

It was after ten, and I knew Eddie wouldn't be home for a few hours—if at all, so I sat down on his bed and scanned the shelves some more. And there, between *The Federalist Papers* and *An American Tragedy,* I found a textbook on abnormal psychology and a few other nonacademic but pertinent titles. I flipped through each of them quickly, but one—*The Culture of Narcissism* (Christopher Lasch, 1979)—I read hungrily.

> Pathological narcissists show a dependence on the vicarious warmth provided by others combined with a fear of dependence, and a sense of inner emptiness. . . . Secondary characteristics of narcissism include pseudo self-insight, calculating seductiveness, nervous, self-deprecatory humor . . .

Sounded familiar.
Ray, I thought.
I read on.

> Chronically bored, restlessly in search of instant intimacy—of emotional titillation without involvement and dependence. . . . these patients, though often ingratiating, tend to cultivate a protective shallowness in emotional relations.

My mouth dropped open.
Ray again. I could suddenly see his face the night he dumped me: impassive, emotionless, contrived.

I put the book down and stared at the bookshelves in amazement.

I dropped to my hands and knees and crawled along the floorboards in front of Eddie's shelves, not knowing exactly what I was looking for but sensing instinctively for the first time that clarity might be close at hand. My eye caught a dusty paperback at the bottom of the last set of shelves: *Men Who Can't Love* (Steven Carter and Julia Sokol, 1987), a cheesy self-help book that looked like it had never been read. I picked it up and opened it to the first page, which had been "dedicated" to Eddie by the giver in big, thick black permanent marker:

THIS IS YOU, the inscription read.

It was signed by someone who must have dated him before I'd moved in since I didn't recognize her name.

Being in Eddie's bedroom, sitting on his bed, on the very blankets and sheets he slept in, holding a self-help book that had been personally inscribed to him by some irate, tortured woman whom he'd obviously driven mad, I felt suddenly like I was at relationship ground zero, about to see a mushroom cloud rise from the bed and blind me momentarily with its gazillion subatomic particles of information.

I opened the book reverentially, and once engrossed, I found pages of fascinating and uncannily relevant descriptions about a subspecies of male human referred to by the author as "commitmentphobics":

> If you have attracted the interest of a commitmentphobic, you will discover that the man changes drastically when a relationship runs the risk of going on "forever."
>
> Typically, the classic commitmentphobic relationship goes through four separate and distinct stages.
> 1. *The Beginning: All he can think about is how much he wants you.*
> 2. *The Middle: He knows he has you, and it scares him.*
> 3. *The End: You want him, and he's running scared.*
> 4. *The Bitter End: It's all over, and you don't know why.*

Me, I thought.

I read on.

> Psychological confinement can be just as claustrophobic as physical confinement, with both representing a loss of freedom. As a result, any serious or lengthy commitment becomes

viewed as a trap, and, like any other trap, it triggers anxiety. The greater the trap, the greater the anxiety and the greater the urge to flee.

What is clear now is that men's reactions to the claustrophobic restrictiveness of commitment are no different than any other phobic reactions. In other words, commitmentphobia is not just a clever catch phrase. *Commitmentphobia is a true phobia,* replete with all of the classic physical and psychological phobic symptomatology.

Ray again.

I closed the book and sat on Eddie's bed for a while, immobilized.

Who was this narcissistic subspecies of men, this *Homo erectus commitmentphobe*?

Just at that moment Evelyn came into the room, whining and pining for Eddie. She climbed up onto the bed and pushed me away as she nestled into the center of his bed and rolled around on her back languorously.

I stared at her.

She was waiting. She was waiting for him to come home.

I looked down at Evelyn and remembered all the nights she'd gotten whipped up into a frenzy when Eddie was around—running after him as he changed his clothes and fixed himself dinner; leaping up onto his pillow and flying into the air repeatedly as he took off his clothes and got into bed to read. Sometimes, as I'd stood in his doorway, I'd seen her rubbing herself all over him, trying to crawl in front of his book and pawing at his private parts as if they were catnip underneath the sheets.

I was horrified, then fascinated.

The next morning at work I felt whacked-out but excited, as if a vision of some great, brilliant psycho-scientific discovery had come to me and taken hold like a religious epiphany. At the office I xeroxed the pages from the books, and later I did a Nexus search on pathological narcissism that yielded a recent article from *Time* magazine. I brought the file of pages into my meeting with Diane and showed her the *Time* piece, which was written by a professor of psychiatry at Harvard. His theory was that pathological narcissism was on the rise and that some of New York's most infamous megalomaniacs had self-destructed because of it. Diane had a weakness for New York megalomaniacs and Harvard professors, I knew, so I wasn't surprised when she gave me her approval to go ahead.

"Book him," she said enthusiastically.

After which, of course, she added: "And where are we with Kevin Costner?"

JOAN MEETS A NEW BULL

A narcissistic patient experiences his relationships with other people as being purely exploitative, as if he were "squeezing a lemon and then dropping the remains." People may appear to him either to have some potential food inside, which the patient has to extract, or to be already emptied and therefore valueless.

—Otto Kernberg, Ph.D.
Borderline Conditions and Pathological Narcissism

·☾ ☽·

THAT NIGHT Joan and I were supposed to have dinner, but in the afternoon she called me at the office and told me she had to cancel. When I asked her why, she said this:

"I'm in love."

I got up from my desk chair and closed my door and ran back to the phone. "In love? Since *when*?"

"Today."

"*Today?*" I said. "With whom?"

"I can't tell you."

"You *can't tell me*?"

"He's kind of famous," Joan whispered.

"Famous," I repeated. "Famous? Like, how famous? Like movie-star famous?"

"No."

"Sports famous?"

"Please."

"Then, how?"

"He's a writer."

Oh, fuck.

"Oh, fuck," I said. "Writers *suck*. They're the worst. I thought we'd both sworn off writers, given our past experience. 'Oh, read this, please, and love it. Love *me*!'" I pleaded, the way Evan and George, two would-be loser short-story writers we'd met at a reading years ago, used to plead.

"I know," Joan said, "but Jason's different. Shit, I said his name."

Different?

She was different. Joan sounded like a pod person, all gooey and sticky and . . . *New-Cow-like.* I tried to refocus on the disastrous matter at hand. "Jason who?"

"Jason Hughes."

Hughes, Jason. "Never heard of him," I pronounced. How famous could he be? "So *tell* me, already."

"Last night I went out with Pat, another editor at *Men's Times,* and she brought along Jason, who's written a couple of stories for the magazine—two of them covers. Anyway, we all stayed out until about three o'clock in the morning. When I got home, the phone was ringing, and it was him calling from his car phone." She made more squeaky pod sounds and went on. "He said he just *had* to call and tell me that it was the most wonderful evening he'd ever had, and then he asked me if he could see me again."

"So then what happened?"

"I said yes, of course."

"I meant, *after* that," I said. *After the truck pulled up in front of your apartment and replaced your body with the giant spotted New-Cow pod.*

"We're seeing each other tonight. And this afternoon, when he called, he asked me to drive out to the Hamptons with him on Saturday. He said he's looking to buy a house and he wants me to come with him. Can you be*lieve* it?"

I didn't answer. I felt the back of my throat get scratchy and then seize up, as if I were about to cough up a hair ball. I was starting to remember all the times Ray had said bullshit just like that, and for a moment I was tempted to tell Joan that Jason sounded just as full of bullshit as Ray had been. But because I couldn't remember the last time she had sounded so happy, and because I knew that part of my reaction was jeal-

ousy—jealousy that she was climbing the arc of passion without knowing about the fall that was coming once she reached
the top—I didn't go whole hog.

"Just be careful," I said.

"Of what?"

"Of, you know, going too fast."

"Oh, like you and Ray?"

"Yeah."

Joan was silent. "For one thing, this is just an affair right
now."

"And?"

"And, for another thing, Jason is different. I mean, this is
different."

No, it wasn't. But I'd said too much already. "So . . . is it
weird?" I asked.

Seemingly relieved to be off that point, she exhaled into the
phone. "Is what weird?"

"Cheating on Ben."

"Ben who?" she said.

Who *was* Ben?

But then, Who was Jason? or, for that matter, Who was
Ray?

As Joan constantly updated me on what was happening
with Jason in the weeks that followed, I'd go home to drink my
beer and eat my toast and think back to what had happened
with Ray. The more she told me and the more I thought about
it, the clearer my sense was that our two situations had a lot in
common: *Homo erectus commitmentphobe.* One night while she
and I were on the phone, I found myself jotting words down
on the pad of paper I kept by my bed:

Same pattern.
Whirlwind courtship.
Instant intimacy.
Extremely romantic verbalists.
Jason asking Joan after first date to see house in Hamptons implied commitment to relationship; Ray telling me after two weeks he wanted to live together implied long-term commitment to relationship.

After we got off the phone, I kept writing.

By 3 A.M. I was out of paper.

The next night, on my way home from work, I went to the drugstore on the corner and bought one of those cheap, fake old-fashioned–looking black and white composition notebooks and got into bed with it and a pen. I wrote and wrote, reconstructing my relationship with Ray—from the first day he came into my office and fixed his hair in my window, to the night at the hair bar, through the summer and into September, when things started to fall apart. I wrote in incomplete sentences (. . . *pursued me* . . . *said "I love you" first . . . made it seem at the end like I was chasing him* . . .), in fits and spurts, and sometimes with bullets and arrows (. . . *breakup with Mia→guilt* . . . *lease signing→panic* . . . *panic→retreat* . . . *retreat→dumping* . . .)—a kind of scientific shorthand, a way of recording a factual account of what had happened, one devoid of feeling or emotion.

The facts. That's all I was concerned with now. Analyses and interpretation would come later.

After that night writing in the notebook became the one thing I actually looked forward to at the end of the day, the one worthwhile thing I could funnel all my obsessive energy into and feel like I was producing something of note:

Notes.

Sometimes, when Eddie was home, we'd eat dinner at the Thai restaurant downstairs that was next to Night Owls and come back upstairs and watch reruns of *The Odd Couple* while I secretly thought about what that night's notebook entry would focus on: Eddie's Current Cow? Jason's latest verbal bouquet? On other nights, when Eddie was out, I'd listen to the country-music station for a while, then shut it off before I started writing so that sentimentality wouldn't creep into my scientific objectivity:

> *Re: Joan's phone call, 10:45 P.M., Jan. 15:*
> *She cooked subject dinner at his apartment. Subject looked at her and said she looked good in his kitchen.*

Or:

> *Ray has cold. Hoping it will turn to flu, then pneumonia. Weeks of bed rest would cause abdominal muscle definition to atrophy.*

Or:

> *Re: Notebooks. Seven filled. Approx. 25,000 words written. Research hours logged: 73. Buy more. Another notebook for me. A separate one to be devoted to Joan. Two to be devoted to Eddie.*

Those notebooks, my database, would, in quite short order, become files—case files—which I filled with newspaper clippings, magazine articles, xeroxed pages from books, and anything else that helped explain why Ray dumped me, why Eddie dumped everyone, why Jason would undoubtedly dump

Joan—and why everything seemed so impossibly, inexplicably fucked up.

Three weeks into the notebook keeping Joan called me at home one night from Los Angeles. She had gone out there to work on the magazine's special West Coast double issue, and coincidentally, she told me, Jason was out there too. She didn't sound as podlike as she had the last time we spoke, so I asked her how things were going with him.

"They're okay," she said. "Actually they're kind of weird. He just got this big assignment from *Vanity Fair* to profile some obscure, small-time royal, and he has to turn it around in three weeks. I guess that would make anyone a little preoccupied and short-tempered, right?"

"And assaholic." I grabbed the notebook marked "J." I could smell another New Cow—one newer than Joan—lurking somewhere in Jason's periphery, and it pissed me off.

Suspect subject has "new" interest, I wrote.

"We're staying in the same hotel, but I haven't seen him since I got here. I keep leaving messages, but when I finally reach him late at night, he tells me he's still transcribing his interview tapes. I mean, how long was the fucking interview?"

Subject using interview transcriptions as excuse for distancing behavior, I wrote.

I could tell she was holding on to her hat and frilly dress for dear life.

"I don't get it. I mean, before we left New York, everything was fine, and when he found out that we were both going to be in L.A., he was thrilled." She paused, and I could hear her pacing back and forth in her hotel room. "Maybe I should try calling again."

"Whatever you do, do *not* call him," I said, writing *DO NOT*

CALL! in big block letters and underlining it three times. "Calling him will only make it worse."

Joan stopped pacing and exhaled into the phone. "This is exactly what happened to you. The minute you and Ray were supposed to move in together, he stopped calling."

I put the notebook down. "That's a tactful way of putting what happened," I said. "But essentially, yes. That's right. He 'stopped calling.' "

"So why is it so hard to see it coming when it's happening to you?"

I closed my eyes, and when I opened them, I saw Ray prancing by my office, looking as happy-go-lucky as he ever had. But I also felt an odd sense of something—relief, probably—that, for the first time since the fall, it seemed that Joan truly understood what I'd been ranting about all those months.

"Uch. I feel sick to my stomach."

"Joan, Joan, Joan," I moaned. "You don't know the half of it."

But she did, unfortunately, get to know all of it over the next few weeks—the unanswered phone calls, the vaporizing of a "love" affair into thin air, the sleepless nights, the obsession. He called her only twice after they came back from L.A., and both times it was to cancel dinner.

Subject appears to be engaging in dash-and-hide method of escape.

It didn't look good.

And it especially didn't look good when Jason's name appeared in boldface on Page Six along with the bluebloods announcing that the two of them were now an item.

Motherfucker! I spat into the notebook that night.

So much for scientific objectivity.

I wasn't ready yet to tell Joan about the notebooks, but the next morning when she called, I couldn't help giving her a taste of my findings on commitmentphobia and pathological narcissism. She was fascinated. Perhaps it was Jason, or the combination of Jason and Ben, but she suddenly seemed to have a voracious curiosity about what I was finding and a renewed interest in Eddie's behavior. Not to mention a truer understanding of me *vis-à-vis* Ray. Night after night I filled her in, and sometimes even during the day, if some late-breaking situation with Eddie warranted it, I would call her at the office, and she would tell her assistant to hold her calls so that she could listen intently and process all the "new" information about men we now had. . . .

FIELD RESEARCH FROM BASE CAMP:
EDDIE MEETS A WIFE

womanizer (woom-e-ni-zer) *n* a man who pursues or courts women habitually; a philanderer

philander (fi-lan-der) *vi* (of a man) to make love with a woman one cannot or will not marry; carry on flirtations

cad (kad) *n* a man who behaves dishonorably or irresponsibly toward women

lothario (lo-thar-e-o) *n* [*Lothario,* seducer in the play *The Fair Penitent* (1703) by Nicholas Rowe] a man whose chief interest is seducing women

Romeo (ro-me-o) *n* 1: the romantic lover of Juliet in Shakespeare's *Romeo and Juliet* 2: any man with a reputation for amatory success with women

Casanova (kaz-e-no-va) *n* 1: Giovanni Jacopo, 1725–98, Italian adventurer and writer 2: a man known for his amorous adventures; rake

Don Juan (don wan) *n* 1: a legendary Spanish nobleman famous for his many seductions and his dissolute life. 2: a ladies' man or womanizer; romeo

Don Juanism *n* SATYRIASIS

satyriasis (sa-te-ri-e-sis) *n* abnormal, uncontrollable sexual desire in a male

·☾☽·

"I SHOULD JUST MARRY this one. She's definitely a wife," Eddie said matter-of-factly, glass of Scotch in hand. He paced back and forth across the living-room floor in front of me the way he always did when he was contemplating the acquisition—or disposal—of a wife:

Step step step turn.

Step step step turn.

Step step step turn.

Not looking up from my copy of *The Social Life of Monkeys and Apes* (Zuckerman, second edition), I feigned indifference. This was not the first time that Eddie had come home from a party and announced that he had met his wife, only to announce two weeks later, without a trace of irony, that he had met another. I'd recorded it all in his notebook:

Case wives: #1–23.

Ages: 22–34.

Preliminary diagnosis of Subject E: satyriasis.

But despite the way of all his previous case wives' flesh and the fact that the chapter on baboons I was reading was a real page-turner, the familiar twinge of curiosity overtook me and I remembered the new purpose of my living arrangement with Eddie:

Research.

Inserting a bookmark in mid-chapter, I approached the cage and threw Eddie a banana:

"So . . ." I said leadingly.

But Eddie didn't seem to hear me, lost as he was in the

stream-of-consciousness comparative-shopping thought processes I now knew by heart:

Step step step great body nice legs good breeding turn.

Step step step but she's a blond ectomorph and I prefer brunette mesomorphs turn.

Step step step she's smart but not smart enough which could be a problem since she has to be smart enough to "get" me which could be difficult as I'm very complex turn.

Step step step what did I do with my cigarettes? Stop.

He frisked himself, and finding a near-empty soft pack of Camel Ultra Lights in the torn breast pocket of his oxford cloth shirt, he shook out a wrinkled cigarette and lit it, then continued his slow, pensive three-step.

Now, where was I? Oh, yes, the question of hair color and whether or not she'll be able to keep up with me intellectually.

I shifted uneasily on the couch.

This excessive pacing and interior monologue was a radical departure from Eddie's usual post-cocktail-party, prenuptial ebullience. If I was going to make the most of his willing—if unwitting—participation in my research, I realized I was going to have to extract the reasons out of him. And while my objective, echoing method of questioning ("It sounds like you're *angry* that she's an ectomorph.") usually achieved maximum results, this time, because memories of Ray and the wanton polygamy of the male stump-tailed macaque I had just read about had made me mad, I said:

"So are you old enough to be her father, or is she at least out of college this time?"

Raising an eyebrow, Eddie acknowledged my reference to his weakness for nubile wives, a weakness that had inspired me, some months back, when I still thought it—and everything else about Eddie's womanizing—was hilarious, to refer to him "affectionately" as Humbert Humbert. But Eddie's finding a wife was serious business these days, and so neither of us was laughing.

"Okay, I'm sorry," I lied. "What's she like?"

Inhaling and exhaling, sipping and pacing, Eddie, as always, considered the question carefully. Hypervigilant in his efforts to capture the true essence of each new wife with precision and accuracy, and in as few words as possible, he said finally, in a tone that implied he had given the question a great deal more than ten seconds of thought:

"She's perfect."

"Perfect," I echoed.

"Well, *almost* perfect," Eddie clarified.

"*Almost* perfect," I echoed again. I was stalling for time. *Almost perfect* was not in the notebook.

"Six inches shy of perfect, to be exact. You see," he said by way of explanation, "she's only five foot one."

The first serious wife contender to come along while I lived with Eddie was the wife he met in early February.

It was a Friday night when he came home and announced his news, parading in front of me in his lucky suit, more than slightly drunk.

"Speak," I slurred.

I, of course, had been sitting on the what-will-become-of-me couch all night, sipping Jack Daniel's daintily from an oversized coffee mug.

He told me that he'd seen his wife at a cocktail party, that she was a cellist, and that she was very beautiful and very rich. In fact, she was *so* beautiful and *so* rich, he said, that he'd found out he would have to get her permission to call her.

"Permission to call her?" I slurred again.

"She's had some unfortunate luck with men," Eddie purred, lighting a Camel and continuing to pace back and forth in front of me. "Luck that I plan to change."

"Good thing you were wearing your lucky suit."

Eddie stared at me. Obviously, at a time like this—post-hunt, prepursuit—he was not in the mood for humor.

"So, what," I said, "you'll call her to ask her if you can call her?"

"No. My friends who had the party will call her. Then they'll tell me if I can proceed."

"*Permission?* How come we don't require permission to be called?" Joan asked when I called her later that night. But before I had a chance to answer, Eddie hit my curtain a few times.

He needed the phone.

An hour or so later he poked his hand through the curtain. *Opposable thumbs up.*

Their first date would be one week thence, Eddie briefed me, the following Saturday night. All weekend long he paced back and forth across the apartment, planning and refining his strategy for the date.

I watched him from my bed through the slit between the curtain and the wall and made notes:

> *Subject E's attempts to pursue "wife" have produced specific feelings of anxiety; convinced that a "perfect plan" for first formal encounter must be executed to produce desired effect in wife object.*
>
> *Subject E grappling intensely with details of said plan (i.e. activity, feeding venue, etc.), as well as with issues of*

*manipulation of wife object's feelings vis-à-vis her percep-
tion of his plan of action.*

*Subject E displaying "deep thought" behavior patterns
but has not verbally communicated to on-site observer.*

Finally, on Sunday night, he filled me in on the details of
his plan: because Catherine had lived her whole life in a rari-
fied environment and undoubtedly missed out on her child-
hood, he would take her to the circus and then to dinner
someplace "common."

Such plotting

Such planning.

Such psychological deconstruction and silent deliberation.

*Bulls become eerily focused when they're formulating their plan
of attack.*

Eddie's date went off without a hitch.

Catherine loved the circus, and she loved the Greek diner
he carefully picked out. The following week he took her ice-
skating in Central Park and to Rumpelmayer's afterward for
hot chocolate and grilled cheese sandwiches. It seemed his
lost-childhood-theme-park strategy was working perfectly.

"Let's celebrate downstairs," he said to me when he'd returned from the date, his Hans Brinker cheeks aglow.

It was only three in the afternoon, and I had never been to
Night Owls in daylight. We sat down at the bar, and before we
had even taken our coats off, our drinks arrived.

I looked at Eddie. "What did you do? Call ahead?"

Eddie took a sip of his Scotch before launching into his
update. "I thought you'd be interested to know that we haven't
slept together yet."

No burying the lead this time.

I stopped in mid-sip. "But you've been seeing her for two weeks. Standard operating procedure for you is normally two hours."

"I know. But this is different. It's *special*," he said, his voice revoltingly full of reverence.

"*Special*?"

"You see," he explained, "sometimes, when a man meets someone special—a wife," he clarified, "it's better to wait. To take things slow." He went on. "You don't want to sleep with a wife on the first date."

I nodded for a few seconds, processing. "But I thought that's what men wanted—to sleep with a woman as soon as possible so that they could fall in love as soon as possible."

Eddie shook his head dismissively. Clearly, I wasn't getting it.

"So you didn't sleep with Rebecca on the first date?" I asked.

He looked past me to the windows that faced the street. "No," he said. "Though she would have."

I looked out at the street too. The air was thick and gray, the way it gets before it snows. "I slept with Ray on the first date," I said, almost to myself. "Maybe that's why it didn't work."

Eddie turned and looked me in the eyes. "No, Jane. It didn't work because Ray's an idiot."

I stared at him. In all the months I'd lived with him he'd never offered an opinion of Ray. His words surprised me. "You think?"

"He doesn't know what he wants yet. He's too young."

Too young.

Ray was thirty. And Eddie was thirty-five. That didn't seem

too young to me to know whether or not you love someone, and what to do about it if you did.

"You need someone older," he continued. "Someone more mature. Someone who can keep up with you."

"Keep up with *me*?" I said. "I'm a fucking mess." I saw my current life flare up in front of me like a lit match and laughed—the hole in my wall, the curtain, the ten-by-fifteen-foot bedroom cell, the notebooks. My life felt suspended in a way it never had: stalled, impermanent, surreal.

"No, you're not. You just fell in love with someone who wasn't ready for it."

I exhaled slowly and closed my eyes, hoping to see in that blackness the glimmer of the future husband that Eddie was describing. But that place was empty, and I didn't want to stay there. I opened my eyes and tried to refocus on the present.

"So what are you going to do about Catherine?"

"We're going to spend the weekend at the Plaza," he said, standing up and leaving a ten-dollar bill on the bar.

I put my cigarette out and slid off the bar stool.

"Bring me back a shower cap, okay?"

Eddie and Catherine never made it to the Plaza that weekend.

The beginning of the end started that Sunday night, after *60 Minutes,* while Eddie was out running.

That's when the phone rang.

"Is Eddie at home?" a female voice said. While I rummaged around the living room for a scrap of paper and a pen, I told the voice that Eddie was out running and that I expected him back momentarily.

"Would you be so kind, then," the voice began again, "as to tell him that Catherine called?"

I scribbled furiously: *Would you be so kind.*

Would you be so kind?

Who talked like this?

It was his wife, being so kind as to call for Eddie for the first time.

I was thrilled for Eddie, then immediately envious. I wished it were a husband calling for me.

Would you be so kind as to tell Jane that I'm completely in love with her?

And then, before I knew it, I was overcome with dread. I had never really considered what I'd do if Eddie actually got involved with someone for longer than a week:

Where would I live?

Who would I talk to?

What would become of me?

Nowhere.

No one.

Nothing.

Sometime later Eddie returned. Momentarily forgetting my impending loserdom, I ran up to him and tugged at his ratty Yale sweatshirt. "Guess who called?" I said, barely able to contain myself. I held the message slip up in front of his face. "*Catherine!*"

He brushed past me through the living room and into his bedroom, removing his running clothes as he went. "Huh," he said, without expression. "I'm going to shower."

Seconds passed.

Minutes passed.

Eddie came out of the shower.

He made rice.

He read the *Sunday Times* cover to cover.

He did the dishes.

Even the silverware.

Then he retreated into his study and closed the door, coming out now and again only to empty his ashtray.

I sat in my room, furious. Three and a half hours had passed since Catherine had called, and still Eddie had not called her back. Just a few weeks before, he could talk of nothing but whether or not she would grant him permission to call her, and now, after two dates and the promise of a third, he suddenly didn't seem to want any part of her.

Finally, when I couldn't take the waiting any longer, I stormed out through the curtain.

"Obviously this isn't any of my business," I said, standing in his doorway, "but when are you going to call her back?"

He looked up at me over his reading glasses and put his pen down, and that's when he said it:

"I just got home."

"You just got home? *You just got home?* What are you talking about? You've been home for three and a half hours!"

Eddie took his glasses off. I waited for him to explain himself voluntarily the way he usually did. But this time he didn't.

"Okay, look," I said. "When you say 'I just got home,' do you really believe you just got home? Is that Guy Time? I mean, does time actually feel different to you? Do three and a half hours really only feel like ten minutes?"

For the first time since I'd known Eddie he looked sheepish. "No," he admitted. "I just don't feel like calling her." He picked up his pen again and put his glasses back on.

Case file closed.

Well, not quite.

I don't know if Eddie ever really did call Catherine back

that night, but I do know that he must have called her eventually, because about a week later he told me they'd had a talk.

"I dumped her," Eddie clarified, looking both ashamed and very pleased with himself, as if he'd managed to unload a beautiful but problematic old Mercedes on an unsuspecting sucker. "She was too stiff, too formal, too uptight."

I imagined her trying to digest the news while he let himself off the hook, like I had when Ray dumped me. The acute misery and confusion of that night and those that followed it pissed me off.

"You're an asshole," I said.

He looked at me like I was kidding. "No, I'm not."

"Yes, you are."

Eddie's face fell slightly as he considered the accusation. "I'm just confused."

"That's the least of it."

I got up off the couch, went into my room through the curtain, and opened up his notebook.

> *Note to the case file:*
> *Wife object dumped.*
> *Subject E exhibiting classic signs of nonempathetic sociopathic behavior.*
> *Prognosis: Ass-holicism.*

THE ORIGINS OF
THE NEW-COW THEORY

The males of most mammalian species have a definite urge towards seeking variety in their sexual partners. If a male rat is introduced to a female rat in a cage, a remarkably high copulation rate will be observed at first. Then, progressively, the male will tire of that particular female and, even though there is no apparent change in her receptivity, he eventually reaches a point where he has little apparent libido. However, if the original female is then removed and a fresh one supplied, the male is immediately restored to his former vigor and enthusiasm.

—Glenn Wilson, *The Great Sex Divide*

·☾ ☽·

IT WAS, BY ALL ACCOUNTS, an inauspicious morning.

In fact, it was just like every other morning I'd had since being dumped.

I woke up before the alarm.

I remembered a dream I'd had about Ray. (*A wild boar was chasing him around the greenroom. Was I the wild boar?*)

I recalled a few choice aspects of our relationship (his washboard stomach, his bad-love-poetry E-mails, his impeccable taste in cheesy vacation souvenirs).

Which made me cry.

Which made me mad.

Which propelled me into the shower, and then to make coffee, and then to sit at the kitchen table smoking cigarettes until I realized that nothing would become of me unless I got dressed and dragged my ass to work.

Little did I know that when I opened the science section of the newspaper at my desk an hour later, I would find the nugget, the germ, the essence of what would become my obsession over the next year: a reference to the mating preferences of bulls buried in an article on human male behavior.

I stared at the article.

My heart pounded.

My breath become shallow.

I started to sweat like Richard Nixon.

I read the article twice, clipped it, stapled it together, then read it again—this time with a yellow highlighter.

The Coolidge Effect was the technical name for it—*it*—the need to provide bulls with multiple cows for mating.

Multiple cows for mating.

I took my reading glasses off, then stood up and checked my watch: forty-five minutes before the production meeting with Diane. I call-forwarded my phone and ran down the hallway to our reference library, small but well stocked, where all PBS staff could do preliminary research on news stories, show topics, and guests.

The Coolidge Effect.

The Coolidge Effect.

I stared at the shelves trying to figure out which books to pull out. I opened the C volume of the encyclopedia and checked under Cattle.

History of the U.S. Cattle Industry.

Cattle Raising.

Domestication.

Breeding Techniques.

See Animal Husbandry.

I scanned the shelves.

A volume missing.

No books on agriculture.

Or farming.

Or animals.

I took a step back and ran my eyes over each section of the shelves—history; politics; psychology; literature; sociology. Finally something caught my eye: The Great Sex Divide (Glenn Wilson, 1989). I lunged for it. As soon as I saw the Coolidge Effect listed in the index, I knew victory was close at hand.

The . . . effect is seen . . . strikingly in farm animals such as sheep and cattle. Rams and bulls are unmistakably resistant to repeating sex with the same female (Beamer, Bermant and Clegg, 1969). Thus for breeding purposes it is unnecessary for a farmer to have more than one male to service all his sheep and cows. A single bull can be relied upon to do the rounds of all the available cows, and a single ram will eventually service all the sheep in his domain.

Unmistakably resistant to repeating sex with the same female. I read on:

Male animals do not choose their mates randomly: they identify and reject those that they have already had sex with. In the case of rams and bulls it is notoriously difficult to fool them that a female is unfamiliar. Attempts to disguise an old partner by covering her face and body or masking her vaginal odors with other smells are usually unsuccessful. Somehow she is identified as "already serviced" and the male moves on to less familiar females.

Already serviced.
New Cow→*Old* Cow.
I stared at the book.
I smiled.
Then I faxed Joan and told her to meet me at Aphrodite for lunch in two hours.

"So, Dr. Goodall. What's the meaning of this cryptic fax?" Joan said, pulling it out of her bag:

New-Cow theory sheds much-needed light on narcissistic behavior in the male species. Stop. Dr. Goodall, disciple of Freud, Leakey, Fossey, and Jung and founder of the Institute for the Study and Prevention of Male Behavior, will present research findings at emergency Aphrodite lunch symposium. Stop. Nota bene: No cameras, please. Stop.

Once Joan had finished scanning it, Dr. Goodall checked the hair in her nonexistent bun. "Yes, you see, my rather busy schedule of research at the Institute and lectures at various conferences around the world about male behavior have, I'm sorry to say, prevented me from transcribing my rather illegible findings into formal papers, and I'm afraid it would do science a great disservice were the press to review my data prematurely—"

Joan lit a Marlboro and looked at her watch. "Come on, Jane. Tell Dr. Goodall to make it snappy."

I pushed the menus aside and leaned forward. "Remember the time I saw that graffiti on the subway?"

" 'Baby I loves the toilet you sit on?' "

"No, no, no. 'I's tired of fucking the same woman every night.' Remember how we thought there might actually be something to that? Like maybe it was some kind of window into their—"

"Schizophrenic behavior?"

"Well, it is," I said, taking out the newspaper. "The New-Cow theory—'I's tired of fucking the same woman every night'—*same thing.*"

I spread the article out on the table and watched Joan read it. Then I showed her *The Great Sex Divide.*

"You see, we were Old Cow," I said, pointing at the book. "We were 'already serviced.' And they wanted to move on to 'less familiar females.' "

Joan shook her head. "I don't know. It's too simple. And besides, that applies to animals."

"So?"

"So . . . you can't extrapolate that the same is true in humans."

"Why not?"

We looked at each other. "Why can't we extrapolate that?" I asked, as much of myself as of Joan.

She thought a minute. "Because. Because humans are more

complex. There are a thousand things that affect what happens between them. This Coolidge Effect or the New-Cow theory is too simple, too one-dimensional. It's much more complicated than that."

"But maybe it isn't," I said, thinking out loud. "Maybe we just assume it's more complicated than that with men when in reality it's something as incredibly obvious as this."

Joan didn't blink. "You really think so?"

"I don't know. It's just something I've been wondering about lately."

In about eleven different notebooks.

"What?" she asked. "Cows and bulls?"

"No." I lit a cigarette and exhaled slowly. "About what the answer is. About why men flip-flop from passion to panic until they finally disappear." I thought about the notebooks and the clippings I'd collected. I thought about Evelyn the cat. And for a moment I was tempted to mention them, to tell Joan more of what I'd been reading and finding. But I didn't. It was too soon—my thoughts were too jumbled, too unformed, the data still too raw.

"Well," Joan said finally. "It certainly would explain Jason."

"And Ray," I said.

We looked at each other, then said the same thing:

"And Eddie."

The weekend after I discovered the Coolidge Effect, I was voracious for information.

Indiscriminate.

Wacko.

I spent the better part of Saturday morning at the Chelsea Barnes & Noble superstore with a store map, winding my way from section to section—Natural History to Psychology to Sociology to Anthropology—picking up books and checking their tables of contents. When something seemed interesting, I took out a special little notebook I'd picked up at Duane Reade on my way to the bookstore—a portable secret spy note-book—and wrote it down:

· *When Mormon crickets mate, male lifts female off ground to see how much she weighs. The heavier the better: more eggs.*
· *Praying mantis: female devours male's head during sex.*
· *Banana slugs: actually hermaphrodites. While mating, males chew each other's penises off.*
· *Eighty percent of all men who die during the act of sex do so while being unfaithful.*
· *Basketball superstar Dennis Rodman's father has twenty-seven children. Father's first name: Philander.*
· *Only three percent of mammals pair-bond.*
· *Ancient Olympic games champion wrestler Milo: after competi-tion reportedly ate entire cow.*
· *First flight by cow in airplane: February 18, 1930.*

Careening around the corner from Aviation, I ran straight into David.

"Hey," he said. "What are you doing here?"

I smiled nervously. "What are *you* doing here?"

"Cruising." He rolled his eyes at the lack of cruise material. "Actually I'm looking for a book on fashion in the forties. Re-search for an upcoming shoe shoot."

I tightened my grip on my mini-notebook and then put both hands behind my back, as if I were stretching. David stared at me.

"What? You look like you've been caught in the act." He

looked me up and down, then opened my coat by the lapels. "Jane? Have you been shoplifting again?"

I laughed as David's hand made its way down my back to where my hands were. I felt him stop at the notebook. He pulled the hand holding it forward. "*Aha,*" he said. "What's this?"

I flipped my hair from one side to the other and played with my earring. "Nothing."

"It's not nothing. It's a notebook."

I tried to pull it toward me, but David had a firm grip. I was getting nervous. "Give it," I said.

He stared at me. "*Give* it?" he mimicked. "How old are you?"

I giggled but pulled hard again on the notebook. "Come on," I repeated. "*Give* it."

He pulled the notebook out of my hand in one clean tug and held it over my head where I couldn't reach it. Then he grinned as he lowered it slowly and opened to the first page.

· *Female hamsters produce sex pheromone in their vaginal fluid: aphrodisin. If smeared onto haunches of male hamster, other males will mount and attempt to mate with him.*

· *Old taxonomic name for chimpanzee was* P. satyrus: *refers to myth of apes as "lustful satyrs."*

· *Sperm count in a husband's ejaculate increases when wife is away—overcompensates for her opportunities to be unfaithful.*

"What is this?"

I shrugged as if I'd just behaved like a twelve-year-old for no reason. "They're just notes."

"I can see that," David said. He flipped the page.

- *Dysthymia: chronic sadness.*
- *Men's brains generally larger than women's. Women use more of their brains than men when they feel sad.*
- *"Mounting behavior in male rhesus monkeys has been induced by electrical stimulation of the lateral hypothalamus and the dorsomedial nucleus of the hypothalamus, leading to coital sequences and ejaculation."*

He closed the notebook. "Notes for what?"

I rifled through my bag, pretending to look for something. "For a show. For a guest for a show."

"Bullshit," he said. "Notes for what?"

I bit my thumbnail. "You wouldn't understand."

"Why wouldn't I understand?" David said. "I understand everything."

I looked at his face and nodded. "Yes. You do." Then I took him by the arm and led him toward the café. "Let's get some coffee."

"I think it's great," David said after I'd told him about the notebooks.

And the clippings.

And the budding case files.

And Eddie and Evelyn the cat and the Coolidge Effect.

"Really?"

"Really." He stirred his coffee. "Let me know what you find out. I could certainly use the information."

"You could?"

"Sure. I mean, it's worse with gay men because you have both of them acting out. At least in straight relationships there's only one man and a woman to diffuse him. I think the reason why so many gay relationships don't work is because there's no woman there to absorb and dilute male narcissism."

"So you don't think I'm insane?"

"I didn't say that. I just think it's interesting. And I also think that whatever helps you get over Ray—whatever makes you feel better—you should do."

Newly anointed monkey scientist not deemed insane. Encouraged by colleague to proceed with research.

"So this science stuff is helping?"

I considered the question. "I guess so. It makes me feel like there are answers, reasons, a bigger picture. When Ray dumped me, all I wanted to know was why. Why, why, why. And he never answered me. He never told me why he did what he did. And I almost think that's worse than the act itself—the not knowing. It's like random violence: All you want to know is what the victim did to bring on the attack so you can prevent it the next time. Was the person in a shitty neighborhood alone late at night? Was the person wearing a big diamond necklace in a shitty neighborhood alone late at night?"

David nodded. "I know what you mean," he said. "But you have to be careful not to replace one obsession with another. Sometimes there aren't answers. Sometimes things just happen. They just *are*."

"Maybe. But I feel like I'm on to something. Like there's something out there that explains it. If I can just find it, if I can just figure it out, I'll be able to get past this. I'll be able to heal straight."

"Well, that's good, then."

We were quiet for a few minutes before I took out my little notebook and leaned across the table like I had a big secret to tell him.

"Did you know that the greater dwarf lemur leaves fecal

scent marks that are sixteen inches long?" I stared at him with my eyes open wide. "Like a big squeeze of *toothpaste*!"

David looked down at his scone and pushed it away. "Extra whitening or tartar control?"

THE BIRTH OF DR. MARIE GOODALL

The Gombe Stream Research Centre grew from small beginnings to become one of the most dynamic field stations for the study of animal behavior in the world. . . . Life at the research centre was busy. In addition to the main business of observing the animals and collecting data, there were weekly seminars at which we discussed research findings and planned ever better ways of collating the information from the various studies. There was a spirit of cooperation among the students, a willingness to share data, that was, I think, quite unusual.

—Jane Goodall, *Through a Window*

·☾ ☽·

JOAN CALLED the next day, on Sunday, to see if I was free in the afternoon to get together. Ben had been out of town all weekend, she said, and she was feeling restless. But after a few more minutes on the phone it sounded like there was more to it than that.

"I've been thinking about our conversation the other day. Your New-Cow theory," she said when I pressed her. "And let's just say I'm ready to consider it now."

I asked her why she had changed her mind, but she wouldn't answer. "I don't want to talk about it over the phone. But if you come over, I'll make pancakes."

Oh-oh.

She always made us pancakes when she was depressed.

I told her I'd be there in half an hour.

"Bring some maple syrup," she said before we hung up. "And bring your file."

Joan was still in her pajamas when I came to her door. Her big white terrycloth hotel robe with the royal-blue Ritz-Carlton insignia (a "souvenir" from an annoyingly long business trip, she'd once confessed) was open, and the belt dragged along the floor. We sat down on the couch and both lit cigarettes before she started to talk.

"Ben's cheating on me." She took a long drag off her cigarette, touched her tongue to her top teeth, then pursed her lips and blew. "He's been away since Wednesday. Said he had to go to London to try to steal an editor away from British *Vogue*."

I stared at her. "So?"

"So. I went in to the office yesterday to catch up on some work. And while I was there, I went into his office to leave him a memo about a few story ideas we had discussed before his trip. And there, on his desk, was this." She held out a small leather-bound booklet. "Can't go to London without your passport."

"No, I guess you couldn't. Are you okay?" I didn't know what else to say.

She shrugged. "No."

"Maybe you're wrong. Maybe it was an old passport?"

"No. I checked." She shook her head. "This isn't the first time," she said softly. "There have been others. This is just the first time his lie has been so *transcontinental*."

"Others?" The only other one Joan had told me about was some freelance writer around a year and a half ago, but none since. And she wasn't even certain she was right. "Why didn't you tell me?"

She sighed and pulled her legs up under her on the couch. "It's completely humiliating, his philandering. I'm sure everyone at the office knows about our relationship, even though we've never 'outed' ourselves and it's supposed to be a secret. And I'm sure everyone knows about him and these other women. I mean, you're supposed to leave someone when they do shit like this, right?"

I shrugged. "I don't know. Not necessarily."

"It's just hard." She reached into her robe pocket for a Kleenex, and I watched as her eyes filled up with tears. "I love him." She blew her nose. "How do you explain that without feeling totally pathetic?"

"I can understand that," I said. And I did. It was the same reason why no matter how much I hated Ray, I still loved him.

"You can? Because I'm not so sure I do." She ran her hands

through her hair, thinking. "It's what I said the other day. We're not animals. We're supposed to have control over our instincts, not act on them just because we feel them. I mean, I'm just as bad. Cheating on him with Jason."

I went into the kitchen to get a bottle of water and came back with it and two glasses. "Do you know who it is?"

"This one? I don't know. Kind of. Who cares? Some new assistant in advertising. It doesn't matter since they're all the same. They're all new. And they're all not me."

I didn't know what to tell Joan to make her feel better. Somehow all the white lies and explanations best friends tell best friends at moments like that seemed hackneyed, useless, false. I felt suddenly like there needed to be another language for comfort:

Science.

Reason.

Logic.

Facts.

I put my cigarette out and reached for the file. "Well, if it makes you feel any better, only three percent of all mammals pair-bond," I said. "Which means that ninety-seven percent of them are—"

"Either fucking New-Cow assistants or the subjects of their magazine profiles?"

I looked up from my file. "That too," I said. "But the word I was looking for was *polygamous.*"

Joan leaned toward me on the couch and tried to read from my file upside down. "But have you found anything more about *why* they're that way? *Why* they say they're in love with us if they're just going to cheat on us?"

I recognized Joan's Old-Cow rage and wished there was something I could say that would alleviate it. But judging from personal experience, nothing short of death of the beloved Bull could do that. I made a sympathetic face and nodded for a few seconds, then turned back to the file with clinical deliberation.

"It has something to do with reproductive opportunities. You know, the more the male mates, the more offspring it can produce. By definition male fitness is the ability to maximize mating frequency."

"Maximize mating frequency," Joan repeated. "But with *different* mates."

"Correct."

I flipped through my articles and the yellow legal pad where I'd scribbled down long paragraphs of notes, then through my secret spy pad from the day before, and found something I was looking for. "Okay, here." I started to read the notes I'd taken from *Sex, Evolution, and Behavior* (Daly and Wilson):

"'Throughout the animal kingdom, males generally woo females, rather than the reverse. This element of the male strategy has been labeled the Copulatory Imperative. As much concerned with quantity as with quality, males are often rather indiscriminate in courtship. . . . Among invertebrates as diverse as butterflies and hermit crabs, males are apt to court an astonishing variety of objects, indeed almost anything that bears some resemblance to a female. The principle also holds up in our own species.'"

"I see," Joan said, standing up and heading toward the kitchen with the Mrs. Butterworth's syrup I'd brought. "So the next time we're stupid enough to fall in love, we have to worry about them cheating on us not only with other women but also with maple-syrup bottles?"

———

No sooner had I gotten home and digested Joan's pancakes than she called me.

"I've been thinking," she said.

A bad sign.

"About what we talked about this afternoon."

Eddie was in the living room watching a John Wayne movie, so I took the phone through the hole and closed the curtain. "Specifically?" I said, reaching for the general file.

"Well, it just sort of clicked after you left. We had a staff meeting last week about an idea someone had that is kind of related."

"Kind of related how?"

"The idea was to add a column in the magazine for women. A column for women about men."

"Really," I said.

"At the time it was going to be about obvious stuff, like how every man thinks he's going bald. You know, like that."

"But why have a column for women if it's a men's magazine?"

"Because girlfriends read it. Wives read it."

Made sense. "I should read it," I said.

I made a mental note to add *Men's Times* to my reading list. It seemed so obvious, I wondered why I had never thought of it myself: reading a magazine specifically targeted at men to find out what and how they think.

"And . . . so?" I said, wondering where this was leading.

"And so after our conversation today I started thinking: *Fuck baldness.* Baldness isn't the issue. The real issue is their behavior—insights into what they do and why they do it. Like the New-Cow theory."

I laughed. "One theory does not a column make, Joan," I said.

"I know. But there must be other things you're finding out that are pertinent."

I glanced over at the pile of notebooks and the file on my little desk. Somehow I didn't think the sixteen-inch fecal trail of the greater dwarf lemur was what she had in mind.

We were both silent for a few minutes. "*Hello?*" Joan finally said, "So, what do you think?"

"About what?"

"About the column?"

I shrugged. "It depends."

"On what?"

I played with the phone cord. "On who writes it."

"Well, a woman would have to write it."

"Obviously," I said. "But you'd have to get a particular kind of woman to write it."

"Right," she said matter-of-factly. I could tell she was pretending to be only mildly interested in what I was saying, but I knew she was staring intently at the split ends on her hair. "Particular how?"

I sat down on my futon and stuffed the pillow between my back and the wall. "She'd have to be smart. She'd have to have been around the block a time or ten. She'd have to have lost her romantic virginity and had it replaced with—" I stopped to try to think of the right word.

"Bitterness?" Joan offered.

"Not bitterness," I said before thinking about it. "Well, yes. I guess she would have to be a little bit bitter." It sounded as absurd as saying someone could be a little bit pregnant.

"In other words, this woman would have to see men for what they really are," she said.

"Right."

Pause.

"Whatever that is," we both snorted.

An hour later, at six-thirty, the phone rang again.

"Believe it or not, I'm in your neighborhood," Joan said. "Come meet me at that disgusting bar you always go to with Don Juan de Eddie."

So I did, and there she was, sitting on a stool with a vodka straight up in front of her and a cigarette already lit. Her eyes widened when she saw me.

I could tell the plot was coming.

I caught the bartender's eye and mouthed the word *Jack* as I sat down on a stool.

"I think you should do it," Joan said.

"Do what?"

"The column."

She was wasting no time.

"Are you crazy?"

"Why?" she asked, as if it weren't obvious.

"*Why?*" I picked up my drink and sucked in a mouthful of thick, undiluted bourbon. "Because."

"Because why?"

My mouth dropped open as I turned to her. "Be*cause*—one, I'm not a writer, and two, I'm not a psychologist."

She waved her hand at me dismissively. "You write fine, and I'm not looking for a psychologist."

"Right. You're just looking for any wacko off the street who's known her fair share of assholes."

"No. I'm looking for someone who's been in the trenches. Someone who gets it. Someone who can communicate that to the multitudes of women who don't." She sipped her drink and shivered. She couldn't get the words out fast enough. "Look, everything you're finding out, everything about psychology and animal behavior and how it explains male behavior—"

"Correction" I interrupted. "Nothing will ever *begin* to explain male behavior."

"I know. But it's something. It's the first time I've ever heard anything that even begins to identify what this—this *thing* is."

"You make this *thing* sound like a disease."

Joan nodded. "Well, maybe it is. I mean, look what happened to you with Ray and what happened to me with Jason. A few things were different, but the essence was exactly the same."

"Hmmm," I said. I knew that, after making the list that night in the notebook.

"So I think we should use it."

"We?"

"You. Me. The magazine. Think of it as providing a service, for which you'll be amply paid."

"But I don't know what I'm talking about, Joan." I flailed my arm out toward the ceiling, and the apartment. "All I have is a bunch of notebooks with unrelated facts and rantings. This isn't a full-time job. It's just a hobby. A sick, twisted, *pathetic* hobby. It's not exactly something I'm proud of, something I'd want to advertise."

"So you'll do it under a pseudonym. You already have one: Dr. Goodall," she said.

"Some pseudonym. Everyone would know it was me."

"No, they wouldn't. We'd just change the first name. To Marie, like Marie Curie. With 'Goodall' conjuring up chimps and scientific observation you've got the perfect composite, impartial, unbiased persona."

I was silent.

Dr. Marie Goodall.

Not bad.

"Look. It's the ultimate revenge fantasy. You get rich and famous writing about something you're already obsessed with. If nothing else it'll be cathartic."

I looked at Joan and then at my drink. I had to admit, it was tempting—the idea of revenge and relief. Like a public flogging. But I told Joan that the prospect of actually pulling it off—doing the research, writing the articles without anyone finding out Dr. Marie Goodall didn't exist—or that she did, and it was me, and even getting *Men's Times* interested in something that would most certainly assassinate the collective ego of the exact gender demographic it was trying to reach—seemed impossible.

"Let me worry about that," Joan said. "First thing tomorrow, when Ben is refreshed after his red-eye back from New Jersey or Queens, I'll pitch the idea to him in the meeting. We'll deal with Dr. Goodall later."

A FRAUD IS BORN

We tend to study animals for what they can teach us about ourselves or for facts that we can turn to our advantage. Most of us have little interest in the aspects of their lives that do not involve us.

—Elizabeth Marshall Thomas, *The Hidden Life of Dogs*

·☾ ☽·

"OPPOSABLE THUMBS UP!" Joan said when she called me at the office the next morning. She had just gotten out of her editorial meeting and was thrilled to report that the staff's response to the idea had been unanimous.

"Most importantly—Ben took the bait," she gloated. "He was practically licking my fingers."

I sat back in my chair, confused. "But why?" I asked. "Why would he want to expose his readers to themselves in such an unflattering way?"

"He said, and I quote, 'Men are narcissistic enough to want to read about themselves no matter what is being said about them.'" She paused a minute for dramatic effect. "See? Aren't you even more convinced about the need for this?"

Kind of.

"But what are we going to do about the fact that Dr. Marie Goodall doesn't exist?" I asked.

"Doesn't exist *yet*. Meet me at my office after work. We'll draft her bio and resumé, and then we'll figure out what to do about a photograph."

I stayed at work until seven-thirty and walked over to Joan's office by eight. When I got there, she shut the door and sat down at her desk.

"Okay. I've made some notes." She turned to her computer and adjusted the monitor so I could see it too. "I picture Dr. Marie Goodall as being somewhere in her sixties—mid sixties. She's foreign, British probably, maybe South African. And she's a doctor of something, though I'd hesitate making her a medical doctor because that might send up a red flag for our fact checkers."

I felt a Nixonian sweating attack coming on but tried to keep it from mushrooming by focusing on why I was doing this.

Why *was* I doing this?

And then I remembered.

Ray.

Jason.

Eddie.

Ben.

Money.

Revenge.

Catharsis.

The sweating subsided. "Born in Sussex," I said.

"Okay." Joan started typing.

"And the degree. Couldn't she just have a Ph.D. in something nebulous, like biology? I mean, does anyone know what Dr. Ruth's degree is in?"

Joan considered the question and typed something into the computer. "Anthropology. And we'll bury that in the body of the bio and resumé, and then we'll load the top with work experience."

We looked at each other and blinked. Like two stupid cows.

"This shouldn't be so hard," Joan said. "Men lie *all the time!* This should be fun!"

Fun.

I was helping concoct the background details of a nonexistent psychologist-*cum*-monkey-scientist-*cum*-professor whose persona I had invented to help me deal with getting dumped and who was about to publish her delusional insights into the male psyche in a national men's magazine.

Joan was right.

This *was* fun. Or, at least, the most fun I'd had since my last notebook entry.

"Okay," I said, determined now to really free-associate. *"Disciple of Freud, Jung, and Erikson. Trained extensively at the University of blah-and-blah"*—I waved my hand at Joan as she typed to indicate that I would fill in those minor details later— *"where she concentrated on clinical research and . . . psychiatric . . . investigation."*

Joan stopped typing. "It sounds like she got her Ph.D. from a police academy."

I looked at her. "Need I actually *say* that all research into male behavior *is* a kind of police investigation?" I asked, but when neither of us answered, we went back to staring at each other, intent on coming up with a better word.

"Exploration," I said.

"Exploration," she echoed, and kept typing. *"Cofounder and director of the Institute for the Study of Pathological Narcissism in Vienna. Lectures extensively around the world about said topic and related topics, including one of her subspecialties, the courtship and mating preferences of farm animals. Currently divides her time between Vienna, Prague, Freiburg, and . . ."*

"Oxford."

"Why Oxford?" I asked.

"It grounds her firmly in academia. Readers love that."

I considered it for a minute and then shook my head. "No. Too big of a lie. Too traceable. It's like saying Harvard or Yale. Let's say Edinburgh instead. That's where Darwin went to school."

"Nice touch."

Joan finished the bio and then went back to the resumé and added some dates and notes to it. Then she printed out a copy of each, and we looked them over.

"We're going to need a photo of her, you know," Joan said.

"A photo?" I looked at her in disbelief. "But that's impossible. Where are we going to find a picture of a sixty-five-year-old woman with white hair and glasses who doesn't exist?"

Joan looked at me, and a smile crept slowly over her face. "Come with me."

I followed her out of her office and down the hallway to a large interior office. Joan flipped on the overhead fluorescent light, and I saw newspapers and magazines neatly stacked everywhere. Above each stack were dates.

"The morgue," Joan said. "Back issues of everything from the past year."

She took a stack of *New York Posts* from one of the shelves and put it down on a big table at the back of the room. We both sat down. "Let's go through the obits," she said, "and see what we come up with."

We went through almost four stacks of newspapers—four months of obituaries—trying to find someone who would fit our fictional description. Finally Joan sat back in her chair and looked at me as if she'd just discovered radon.

"Look," she whispered, and pointed to a photo.

I got up from my chair and went around to her side of the table. I bent down and looked at the grainy photo and saw what Joan had seen. "Dr. Marie Goodall," she whispered again. "*Definitely* Dr. Goodall."

I agreed. "It's unbelievable. She's perfect."

"She's exactly what we've envisioned."

I stared at the photograph, awestruck. "She looks so . . . scientific . . . and trustworthy. She even has a bun."

"And once we make a few alterations, no one will ever know she's the recently deceased Edith Gold of Astoria."

Our next stop was the art department, where Joan showed me something she said was called the Scitex machine. If we fed the photo into it, she explained, we could alter the features of the face slightly and make her less recognizable. Apparently all the women's magazines used the machine to make the models' faces and bodies even more perfect than they already were, and at *Men's Times* they used it to enhance men's muscle definition.

Joan fed the photo into the scanner and looked at it on the screen. Using the mouse, she thinned the lips, raised the eyebrows, thickened the nose, and little by little the features of the face changed so that when we held the two photos side by side, they looked different enough.

"Like sisters," I said.

Joan turned off the scanner and shut off the lights, and we took the photos back to her office.

"Tomorrow I'll go through the software manual and figure out how to add a white lab coat."

I took one last look. "And a stethoscope."

The next day Joan went to Ben and proposed Dr. Marie Goodall as the writer for the *Animal Husbandry* series. She showed him the bio, resumé, photo, and a list of possible topics, and he approved the contracts. One article would have to be delivered at the end of February to run in the May issue, she said when she called me at the office, and if it got a good reception, a second article would have to be delivered in March for the June issue. Our deadline schedule: one week to decide on the topics for the first article and two weeks to research and write it. Joan's only stipulation was that she wanted the article to start with the New-Cow theory, commitmentphobia, and pathological narcissism. The rest would be up to me.

"I mean, up to Dr. Goodall," she corrected herself.

We'd go over my ideas on the weekend, and until then, she said, I should read everything I could get my hands on.

Little did she know my notebooks were overflowing. But I felt I hadn't even begun to scratch the surface.

"Immerse yourself," she said. "We'll edit later."

THE ONSET OF MAD-COW DISEASE

"It was the twenty-fifth of April 1985," veterinarian [Dr. Colin Whitaker] remembers, "when one of my dairy clients phoned up to say he'd got a cow behaving oddly and would I come and have a look at it." Whitaker drove to Plurenden Manor farm outside Ashford, in central Kent. . . . One of the Plurenden Manor Holsteins was sick. "When you approached her," Whitaker recalls, "she would shy away. She was previously a quiet cow and had started becoming aggressive, rather nervous, knocking other cows, bashing other cows and so on and becoming rather danger-ous to handle. . . ."

> —Richard Rhodes, a chapter on mad cow disease in
> *Deadly Feasts: Cracking the Secrets*
> *of a Terrifying New Plague*

·☾ ☽·

FOR THE NEXT WEEK I lived a double life: Jane Goodall, distracted talk-show talent booker, by day ("*Who* died?" "A terrorist bomb went off *where*?"), and Dr. Marie Goodall, delusional fraudulent obsessive monkey scientist, by night.

Every day I'd rush home from the studio, make a little small talk with Eddie, and after he'd go out, I'd get to work, poring over the books and magazines I'd bought or brought home from the library, searching for something that would lay bare the secret workings of the human male heart and mind.

No small task.

I read Freud and Jung and Skinner.

I read Darwin and Margaret Mead and Richard Leakey and the real Jane Goodall.

I read about oral cravings and anal fixations and separation anxiety, about natural selection and sexual selection and courtship and mating rituals in birds, fish, mammals, primates, and humans.

I watched *Nova, Nature, Wild Kingdom,* and *Love Connection.*

I read *Time* and *Newsweek, Natural History, Scientific American, Discover, Nature,* the science section of *The New York Times; Nature Genetics, GQ, Esquire, Cosmopolitan, The Farmer's Almanac* and, of course, *Men's Times.*

And as I did, I thought and contemplated and theorized and analyzed.

And I wrote and wrote and wrote.

Not just about the particulars of primate copulation, for instance (though I did become quite fascinated by this subspecialty: *brown-headed spider monkey: mating lasts for 5–10 minutes; chacma baboon: 3–11 minutes; dusky titi monkey: 10–30 seconds*), but about anything and everything that struck me as interesting, potentially relevant, annoying, or just plain weird.

Like the fact that three months of back issues of the *Science Times* yielded thirty-one existing and emerging scientific sub-specialists all very hard at work trying to figure out the complexities of human behavior, including evolutionary psychologists, medical anthropologists, psychobiologists, and fish scientists.

Or that an elephant's vagina is called a *vestibule.*

Or the extremely irritating wire-service item about Stephen Hawking, author of *A Brief History of Time,* which reported that he had married his nurse, one of fifteen such helpers who take care of him (read: feed him, bathe him, wipe him, change him). Item also reported that Hawking married said nurse after a twenty-six-year marriage to his first wife.

(Can I just say?

Hawking is a quadriplegic?

A twisted, contorted, immobile *man*?

If he were a woman, he would never have gotten married *once,* let alone *again.*)

Or a *Newsweek* article that described recent experiments conducted to map the brain differences in men and women. The study showed that when both sexes were presented with photographs of facial expressions and asked to determine what emotion was being expressed, women were able to correctly identify a sad face ninety percent of the time on men and women. Men, of course, had more trouble with this. While they could correctly identify sadness on *men's* faces ninety percent of the time (big surprise), they had a seventy-percent success rate when it came to identifying sadness on *women's* faces. In addition PET scans revealed that men used significantly *more* of their brains during this exercise than women did, and they *still* got fewer answers right.

And, one of my favorites: an article from the *Washington Post* which reported that "most mammals actually have two 'noses' for sensing odors: the familiar, visible one, which responds to a broad spectrum of odors in the environment; and the 'erotic' nose, or vomeronasal organ, a specialized structure hidden near the base of the nasal cavity in reptiles and in most mammals, which responds only to pheromones." This "erotic" nose is not related to areas of the brain that control higher functions but to the amygdala, a primitive part of the brain that mediates emotions.

Such provocative though somewhat unrelated findings as those just mentioned gave me a lot of ideas, and sometimes, in between tomes and scientific journals and factoids, I would jot down a follow-up reminder like this in my own personal notebook:

> *Sense memories of Ray remain persistent. Scent triggers include: soap, fresh laundry, and Obsession—Calvin Klein's Obsession. Call American Society of Plastic and Reconstructive Surgeons to find out whether vomeronasalectomy surgery is available.*

THE MAKING OF ARTICLE I

While female chimps form only casual bonds, female bonobos establish lifelong relationships, spending much of their time socializing with one another and even engaging in recreational sexual activity together.

"For [male bonobos] with an aggressive bent, such a powerful sisterhood spells trouble. If a sexually mature bonobo male shows a female unwanted attention, she has merely to sound a distress call to bring an avenging group of females quickly to the scene. Males that misbehave in a nonsexual setting—say, at a feeding site, where they may try to hoard a cache of fruit and prevent other troop members from approaching—are similarly intimidated or chased off.

Time, October 14, 1996

·☾ ☽·

BY THE TIME Saturday morning rolled around, I felt like my head was going to explode.

"I'm leaving," I heard Eddie say from the living room.

I looked up. I hadn't eaten since lunch the day before, let alone showered. My hair was falling out of its bun, and I pushed my glasses back up my nose. I couldn't remember the last time I'd actually seen Eddie—sometime after Freud but before Leakey, I guessed.

I opened the curtain just enough to expose my face. "Leaving?" I said. "For where?"

He was wearing old khakis, a white T-shirt, and canvas basketball sneakers. Weekend wear.

He stared at me. "East Hampton."

"Good. Good. Who with?"

"My new wife."

"Good. Good."

His mouth dropped open. "Aren't you going to ask me who she is?"

I adjusted my glasses and smiled absently. "Nope. Nope. I'm sure she's lovely, whoever she is. Just have a good time."

"Wait," he said as I started to close the curtain. "What's wrong with you? What have you been doing in there every night this week?"

"In where?"

"In your bat hole."

"I'm just, you know, working."

"Working? On what?"

"Something . . . for . . . Diane," I mumbled. "A special project. A special thing she asked me to do. Big rush on it."

He lit a cigarette and put his hands on his hips. "Tell me, Jane, or I'll come in there and find out." His voice was low, faux-threatening.

"Okay, okay," I said, taking my glasses off. "But don't tell Diane I told you." I paused for effect and to think of a lie. "You know her thing about Kevin Costner?"

He nodded.

"Well, she wants me to write a special letter to him. Kind of like a proposal." I had no idea what I was talking about, so I just kept going. "A package to send to him with videotapes and other material to try to convince him to come on the show. A *pitch,* if you will."

"But that's what you do—at work."

Or what I *should* do at work.

I shook my head with an air of secrecy and condescension. "No. Not like *this.*"

He put his cigarette out and picked up his bag. "Well, okay. I guess I'm off—off to elope with my new wife about whom you know nothing," he said as he walked down the hallway to the front door.

I closed the curtain. "What*e*ver."

Before I showered and washed my hair, I called Joan and told her to come over. And an hour later she did, arriving exactly when she said she would—at ten-thirty—a first for her in the arena of punctuality.

She looked at me expectantly. "Speak," she said.

So I told her about male bowerbirds, who build elaborate nests and decorate them to attract females.

About the underwater love songs of male dolphins.

About how monkeys and dogs and even butterflies can smell out receptive females from miles away because of the allure of pheromones.

I told her how sexual behavior in humans goes through three distinct phases—pair formation, precopulatory activity, and copulation—but not necessarily in that order.

About how flies and birds lure females by giving them a nuptial offering of food to eat while they mate, and how often-times the male will take back the uneaten portion once their mating is complete so he can use it to attract more females.

And then I told her some of my half-gelled theories.

"You know how uncanny it is that there are so many simi-larities in the way men dump women? The things they say, the words they use, the order in which everything unfolds?"

Joan nodded. "Like Ray and Jason."

"Not to mention Eddie."

She nodded again.

"There's an obscure term I came across which could explain it: *allelomimetic behavior.*"

Joan moved her lips and tried to pronounce it, but she couldn't. I showed her the copy of the page from the scientific dictionary and then I read the definition out loud: " 'Of or characterized by imitativeness within a group: All the sheep in a flock, or all the fish in a school, or all the dogs in a pack, tend to do the same thing at the same time.' "

She looked at the piece of paper and then at me. "It's like how all alien abductees draw the same picture of the alien that abducted them! As if it's somehow part of the collective uncon-scious."

"Right. Or like how all men seem to have gone to school

and taken some secret *break-up class*," I said, "because they all say and do the same thing when they end a relationship, as if they were—"

"Genetically programmed."

I flipped through the file and showed her another piece of paper. "Did you know there's actually a word for the love of new things? It's called *neophilia.*"

I flipped again and found a cover story from *Time* called "*The Chemistry of Love.*" "And because falling in love produces amphetaminelike chemicals, some people, and I quote, '*move frantically from affair to affair just as soon as the first rush of infatuation fades*' and become *attraction junkies.*"

Finally I told her about the different methods of escape animals use—freezing, fleeing, zigzagging, the dash-and-hide, the dash-and-retreat.

"So I'm focusing on the two topics you specified, and I'm going to add allelomimetic behavior and something I've been working on called the myth of male shyness, if you think that'll work."

Joan nodded. "That'll work."

Then I asked her to look at a very, very rough draft of the article I'd done, just to make sure Dr. Goodall was on the right track. Joan stared at the batch of yellow legal paper I'd ripped from the pad intently and silently, letting the pages drop onto the floor one by one as she read them.

"Yes," she said. "I like this track. This is a good track. Keep going on this track."

So I did.

I spent the rest of the weekend writing, and on Monday morning, when I got to the office, I faxed Joan the complete article. We went over it that night on the phone so she could take it with her in the morning to her editorial meeting.

She called me immediately afterward.

"All the women in the room went crazy," she said excitedly. "And when the meeting was over, we all went into the bathroom and smoked and traded war stories. The world is one big fucking Used-Cow lot, it seems."

"What did Ben think?"

Joan laughed. "He looked *chagrined*. As if he'd just read the first chapter of his unauthorized biography."

I present the article herewith in its entirety:

ARTICLE I:

THE OLD-COW–NEW-COW THEORY ALLELOMIMETIC BEHAVIOR, AND THE MYTH OF MALE SHYNESS

A <u>MEN'S TIMES</u> EXCLUSIVE

When MEN'S TIMES photographer Zoe Raider went to shoot DR. MARIE GOODALL, she found a small, absentminded woman wearing a white lab coat and a high-intensity examination light bulb strapped to her forehead, sitting behind her large, messy desk, looking as if she were waiting for a PBS documentary film crew to arrive. The office, with its faded diplomas, Bunsen burners, beakers, taxidermied apes and monkeys, walls of textbooks, and, of course, obligatory analysis couch, looks like it could belong to a psychologist, professor, or monkey scientist—and indeed DR. GOODALL considers herself to be all three. Dwarfed by the stacks of files and papers in front of her—the hundreds, if not thousands, of documented "cases" of male behavior she has studied during the course of her thirty-five-year career—DR. GOODALL sits on the edge of her chair, excited at the opportunity of discussing her theories for the first time.

NOTE TO THE READER FROM DR. MARIE GOODALL:

When this male-oriented magazine contacted me to write about the human male, I was rather surprised—not only by the fact that the editors were aware of my existence as a recognized expert in the study and prevention of male behavior but also by the fact that they felt there was an apparent and somewhat urgent need for my findings and theories to appear in a general-audience publication. Whilst I have written a great many papers over the decades on this subject, I have, I must admit, written only for scientific journals. Allow me, then, to apologize in advance for the rather technical and clinical manner in which I address these topics.

And so, let us begin with the Old-Cow–New-Cow theory, Allelomimetic Behavior, and the Myth of Male Shyness.

THE OLD-COW–NEW-COW THEORY

The occurrence of a male tiring of his current female mate and leaving her for a new female mate is certainly not an aberrant occurrence in either the human kingdom or the animal kingdom, though it is far more accepted in the latter. While it is commonly known that most animal species are not monogamous (only three percent of mammals are categorized as such, in fact), and that their polygamy runs rampant at times, what is rarely known is just how rampant it is. Knowledge of this phenomenon as it appears in the animal kingdom should, I trust, help the human female comprehend the phenomenon when it manifests itself in her own backyard, as it were.

Perhaps the clearest example of this can be found in the Coolidge Effect. If I may digress for just a moment, I generally like first to share with my students the rather amusing anecdote that gave the phenomenon its name before describing the particulars of the phenomenon itself. According to one of my favorite texts available on this topic, *The Great Sex Divide* by Glenn Wilson, the phenomenon was named as such as a result of an incident involving President and Mrs. Coolidge:

> The story goes that President and Mrs. Coolidge were visiting a government farm in Kentucky one day and after arrival were taken off on separate tours. When Mrs. Coolidge passed the chicken pens she paused to ask her guide how often the rooster could be expected to perform his duty. "Dozens of times a day," was her guide's reply. She was most impressed by this and said, "Please tell that to the President." When the President was duly informed of the rooster's performance he was initially dumbfounded. Then a thought occurred to him. "Was this with the same hen each time?" he inquired. "Oh no, Mr. President, a different one each time," was the host's reply. The President nodded slowly, smiled and said, "Tell *that* to Mrs. Coolidge!"

The Coolidge Effect as it applies to the mating practices of sheep and common dairy cows is known by veterinary scientists and cattle breeders the world over, which is why farmers need have only one male to service all their sheep or cows: *male resistance to repeating sexual contact with the same female.*

The details of the phenomenon were recounted in a landmark study by the researchers Beamer, Bermant, and Clegg in 1969:

On Day I of the study researchers presented a bull with a cow. Mating ensued.

On Day II of the study researchers presented the bull with the same cow. Mating this day did *not* ensue.

On Day III of the study researchers presented the bull with the same cow that had been visually disguised (data is inexact on precisely what was used to achieve this effect—most probably women's clothing and undergarments in rather large sizes or a very big paper bag placed over the head). But again mating did not ensue.

On Day IV of the study researchers realized the bull was resistant to deceptive visual stimulus and proceeded to disguise the cow in a different manner: they smeared the vaginal odor of a fresh cow onto the vaginal area of the previously mated cow. While the bull's interest was momentarily piqued, mating again did not ensue.

Undeniable hypothesis: The bull desired a *New* Cow and would *not* mate twice with what he perceived to be the *Old* Cow.

With human males and females the Coolidge Effect manifests itself in a subtler though still apparent way. Most commonly it occurs when a male, after engaging in a romantic and sexual relationship with a female for a period of time—a month, three months, six months, a year or more—grows increasingly bored with his previously New Cow. In the vernacular this is usually referred to as the "itch." The male will then begin to sniff around, if you will, for variety and will pick from the somewhat wide selection of New Cows available to him one to his liking. Mating with this New Cow will ensue, which will promptly lead him to view the Cow he is primarily involved with as his Old Cow. In the majority of cases the male will leave the Old Cow to pursue a relationship with this New Cow, only to find, after a varying period of time, that this New Cow has gotten Old, and he will desire variety again and so repeat this process innumerable times. At present writing there is no set cure for this Old-Cow–New-Cow syndrome in either animals or humans, though my institute is working quite diligently in this pursuit.

ALLELOMIMETIC BEHAVIOR

This is a little known but crucial concept for the understanding of human male behavior. *Allelomimetic behavior* refers to the curious phenomenon observed when animals inexplicably behave in exactly the same way—that is, mutual mimicking: One group member does something, which leads another to do the same thing, and because others are now doing what the first one started doing, that first one continues. Birds in a flock fly together; fish in a school swim together; sheep and cattle in a herd follow one another, etc. The prevailing assumption at work here is that some intuitive and innate impulse produces the particular behavior in the first group member, and the allelomimetic impulse induces the others to follow suit.

In human males this principle is manifested quite often—most clearly in courtship and wooing methods used to attract females, as well as fleeing and abandoning strategies used to dispose of them. In fact, allelomimetic behavior is so frequent and obvious in males that many females experienced in the ways of men have come to know that such a principle is at work, even if they are unaware of the scientific name for it.

At present writing there too is no set cure for allelomimetic behavior in either animals or humans, though again my institute is working quite diligently in this pursuit.

THE MYTH OF MALE SHYNESS

I feel I must also comment on the very interesting and common myth of shyness in the male species, as it is one that has fascinated me, and many of my colleagues, I might add, for quite some time.

It is a rather curious phenomenon that usually manifests itself at the onset of a romantic relationship, when the male exhibits a series of convincing behaviors suggesting that he is, in layman's terms, shy. The behaviors in question are quite common ones—awkwardness, trepidation, disbelief that the female has taken an interest in him—that do-I-dare-to-eat-a-peach demeanor, as T. S. Eliot so accurately described it, though it must be acknowledged that he was a notorious narcissist himself.

I have studied many such cases in the course of my research, and in each one a similar pattern has emerged: At the beginning of the romance the male is shy; at the end of the romance the male is *not* shy. In fact, if I may digress for just a moment, I observed this rather curious personality transformation firsthand once, many years ago, when I began my research. I was being pursued by a young chimp who seemed at the time (as I was not trained to recognize and diagnose the behavior as I am now) to be genuinely shy. The courtship progressed, as it were, and once he was assured of my continued presence, he quite suddenly—and unshyly, I might add—displayed that he no longer wished to see me.

Naturally I was absolutely confounded by the abrupt change in his behavior, though luckily, of course, I was in the wild, where I had immediate and unlimited access to a large group of chimpanzees in whom I observed this rather subtle phenomenon time and time again. And it was this incident that compelled me to embark on the course of my life's work: observation *and* prevention.

And so, yes, while the male does indeed seem shy—or, to be more precise, insecure—he is actually a narcissist in monkey's clothing, because this apparent shyness belies the much more serious and deeply rooted feelings of unworthiness, low self-esteem, and fear of rejection. And *these* are the feelings that motivate the narcissistic male—*this* is what causes him to crave love and *this* is what compels him to seek attention from New Cow after New Cow *ad nauseam et infinitum.*

Now that the article was finally finished, I applied myself to my day job.

I pursued Kevin Costner's agent and team of publicists with renewed vigor—actually preparing and sending the pitch packet I had described to Eddie.

I ignored Ray, even when he would sit down in my office and try to be funny (*"Do you think Diane had her chin done in St. Bart's?" "Do you think she's forty-two or sixty-two?"*) or cop a few warm and fuzzy feels (*"Remember Wellfleet? Do you still have that bar of lobster soap I bought you?"*). I had gotten wise to his seeping attention-extracting ploys that never led anywhere and refused to acknowledge them—except in my notebook:

R displayed "conciliatory" behavior by referencing past romantic interludes. Monkey scientist showed no external reaction and felt great pride at her emotional progress.

Or:

Fecal verbal trail left behind by R was not followed by dupable female monkey patsy.

And I resumed watching Eddie again, though since I'd read about the Heisenberg uncertainty principle—the theory that an observer can have an inadvertent effect on the observed—I tried to be less intrusive and to keep my questions to a minimum.

At the end of the week, just when I was about to call Joan at the office to tell her about yet another variation of egregious dumping by Eddie (the default dump—dumping by nonresponse), the phone rang before I had even dialed it.

"I had to call you," Joan said breathlessly. "The article sparked such a debate at the office all week that we're running it early. Ben killed a piece on the new monogamy, and we're rushing Dr. Goodall into the April issue. Isn't that fabulous?"

I sat down on my bed. April was right around the corner, and I hadn't even dealt with the reality of the article being published in the first place.

"The timing couldn't be better. It'll be on stands practically on the first day of spring," she said. "We'll show those pathological romantics who fucking *rules*."

EDDIE'S NEW-COW–OLD-PIG STORY

In a recent study, Dr. Patricia Pliner, a social psychologist at the University of Toronto, found that women who eat less are considered more feminine by both men and women, regardless of the woman's body weight. A man's masculinity was unaffected by how much he ate.

"Food is used as an impression management technique," Dr. Pliner said. "If a woman wants to appear feminine, if she is in the presence of an attractive male she will eat less than if she is in the presence of an unattractive male or another female."

The New York Times, March 2, 1994

·☾ ☽·

    Case wife: #379
    In re: Twenty-one-year-old Barnard senior underage victim du jour.
    Status: Dumped.
    Cause of Subject E's behavior: Nonspecific feelings of anxiety and repulsion.

"So what was it this time?" I asked. "Too beautiful? Too smart? Too rich? Too almost-perfect?" It was a Sunday night about a week after I'd finished the article, and Eddie had just returned from another weekend in the country with his new wife. At least by now I'd seen her—when she came by on Friday evening to pick him up—though I didn't feel the urge to know her name since, given Eddie's track record, I knew she wouldn't be around long. Needless to say, she was beautiful.

Eddie pretended to ignore me, but I could tell he was as perplexed by the latest cessation of his husbandly feelings as I was. So I sat down on the couch and watched him pace, preparing to open my direct examination.

"You went to a movie," I stated.

"Correct."

"Then you went back to the house."

"Correct."

"And . . . ?" I said leadingly.

Eddie lit a cigarette and paced evasively. At first I couldn't understand why he submitted to these postmortems, which were always unpleasant for him, not to mention disappointing, since they underscored his growing suspicion that he would never find a perfect wife to replace Rebecca. But as my expertise in the field of pathological narcissism grew, the answer became perfectly clear: Eddie participated in these discussions because they were about Eddie. This particular postmortem was especially disappointing, he told me, since he'd really thought she might be The One.

"And, we went into the kitchen to get something to drink. We'd had dinner after the movie, but she was still hungry. She's always hungry, it seems."

Always hungry. I folded my arms across my chest. I remembered her standing in the living room with her car keys in her hand: tall, thick dark hair, definitely a mesomorph.

Check.

Check.

Check.

Oh, *fuck* the Heisenberg uncertainty principle.

"Is that bad?" I asked. "Women who eat? I mean, she's not fat."

"No, she isn't fat," he said, perplexed. He continued to pace.

"Okay, so you're in the kitchen. And she's hungry—*again.* Then what happens?"

Eddie exhaled loudly. "Well, we were standing there, and she opened the refrigerator and took out a pint of Häagen-Dazs. And she started eating it out of the container. And, I don't know, there was just something about it that made me think things weren't going to work."

I stared at him. "Was the refrigerator door open?"

He looked bewildered. "Why?"

"Was the refrigerator door *open* or *closed*?" I repeated, trying to keep my voice from rising into hysteria. "Just answer the question."

Eddie stared at his cigarette. "It was open, I think."

I crossed my legs underneath me and sat up straight on the couch. "Would it have made a difference if the door was *shut*? Would *that* have made the act of a *not-fat woman eating ice cream out of the container a little less revolting*?"

Eddie looked at me like I was insane.

"Would it have made a difference if she *hadn't* just eaten dinner? If she had instead been *legitimately* hungry when she *shoved her face into the trough of Häagen-Dazs*? Would it have *repulsed you less* if she'd put the ice cream into a *dish*?"

Eddie stubbed his cigarette out midway and went into his room. I leapt off the couch and chased after him to ask what flavor the ice cream was, but it was too late. He slammed the door in my face.

"Good night, you psycho," I heard him say jeeringly through the door.

"Good night, you *neophiliac,*" I said back.

I went to sleep that night satisfied that we were both, finally, properly diagnosed.

DR. MARIE GOODALL:
MAD MAGAZINE MONKEY SCIENTIST

A terrified calf bolted from a delivery truck and ran rough-
shod over a Bronx neighborhood yesterday morning before
Emergency Services cops lassoed her and returned her to a
nearby live-poultry market.

Within hours, USDA inspectors and ASPCA enforce-
ment officers returned to The Bronx's Live Chicken Market
to seize . . . the calf. . . .

"The truck pulled up and . . . the cow tore off in the
other direction," said Officer Glenn Dowd of the 47th Pre-
cinct. "I guess she knew where she was and she didn't want
to go inside."

The New York Post, May 22, 1997

·☾ ☽·

Dateline: February 15. New York City.

Joan and I sat in her office, beaming at an early copy of *Men's Times.*

"Look at this," she said, flipping the pages. "The art department really outdid themselves. Look at this great picture they found of cows grazing. And look how well Dr. Marie Goodall came out." She pointed to the contributor's page where there was a little-bigger-than-postage-stamp-sized Dr. Goodall, peering out kindly, but wisely, from her obituary pose.

We read the article silently from start to finish, and then we looked at each other.

Blink. Blink. Blink.

Copies would be on newsstands nationwide by the end of the week.

Dateline: February 22.

The following week, a few minutes before I had to go into a meeting with Diane, Joan called.

"Are you sitting down?"

"No, I'm just on my way into—"

"Sit," she said.

So I sat.

"The phone has been ringing off the hook all day. We've gotten three hundred letters, mostly from women, and we haven't even seen today's mail or E-mail from our Web site. Everyone wants Dr. Goodall."

"What do you mean 'wants'?"

Joan lit a cigarette and rustled through the papers on her

desk. "*Oprah* called. *The Today Show* called. *Good Morning America* called. *Larry King. Geraldo.* CNBC. CNN." She rustled some more and continued. "*USA Today,* the *Chicago Tribune,* the *Boston Globe, Miami Herald, L.A. Times.* Everyone wants an interview. Not to mention book publishers and literary agents. They're calling this the Nuclear War of the Sexes."

Diane poked her head into my office, but I rolled my eyes and mouthed the words *Kevin Costner's publicist.* She nodded excitedly and disappeared. I closed the door and swiveled my chair toward the window.

"*Fuck!*" I whispered. "This wasn't part of the plan."

"I know," Joan said. "I mean, I knew we'd get *some* letters, and *USA Today* calls about everything, but I never thought we'd be deluged like this."

"*Fuck!*" I whispered again. "What are we going to do?"

"There's nothing we *can* do. Obviously Dr. Goodall is 'unavailable for interviews.' That's what I keep telling our PR department every time they buzz me. '*She's shy,*' I say. '*She's reclusive.*' '*She's in Vienna.*' '*She's in Paris.*' '*She's at a conference in Tangiers.*' "

"Tangiers?"

"Hey, these talk-show Nazis will go almost anywhere to track down someone they want. You should know that."

Diane poked her head in again, and I told Joan I had to go. Then I raced down the hallway to the greenroom and sat next to Eddie and across from Ray and Evelyn, who were sharing a legal pad and agenda because he had forgotten his.

What an idiot he was.

Diane looked at me expectantly. "So what's the word on our Kevin?"

I looked down at the one word on my pad and shook my

head sadly. "We just missed him." I sighed. "He's in, um, Tangiers."

"I shouldn't have used up Tangiers on fucking Kevin Costner," I told Joan the next day. It was after five, and I was tired and cranky. My nerves were frazzled. The pressure was getting to me.

Joan laughed.

"Hey, this isn't funny! Diane spent the entire meeting reading passages from my article, saying how accurate everything was, going by her own 'research' with men. She kept repeating *'Get me this New-Cow doctor! Get me this New-Cow doctor!'* over and over, and then she sent Eddie back to his office to start digging."

I heard Joan's other line ring, and she told me to hold.

"It's Don Juan de Eddie, sniffing around about Dr. Marie," she said, breathless. "This is going to be fun. I'll call you back."

An hour later, at six, I put my coat on and swung by Eddie's office to see what, if anything, he'd found.

"Any luck with Dr. What's-her-name?" I asked.

Eddie looked up from his cigarette-butt-covered desk and rubbed his eyes. "No, not yet. I spoke to your friend Joan today, though, and she's messengering over a bio and photo. Maybe that'll give me some leads to follow."

I sat down in his guest chair and tried to appear disinterested. It wasn't easy.

"I called Joan too. But she said this 'doctor' never gives interviews. Spends all her time researching. And besides, she's based in Europe."

Eddie turned off his computer and picked up his pack of cigarettes and bag as we left his office. "I hope this doesn't turn into another Kevin Costner thing."

———————

Luckily for me after a few days, Dr. Marie Goodall was already starting to be old news to people in the business. Diane gave up the chase, albeit reluctantly, along with everyone else in the media. At Friday's meeting Eddie was taken off Dr. Goodall's scent. Joan, however, was not so lucky. Ben was tormenting her in and out of the office. He simply could not believe that Joan was unable to get Dr. Goodall into even one interview. How could she not find her star columnist? They were missing an opportunity to sell even *more* magazines. When would her next six columns be ready? Joan placated him by holding out the promise of an America Online chat session with Dr. Goodall. She wasn't sure how long she could stall Ben, but this seemed to be working for now.

Ray and I left the greenroom together and walked down the hallway without speaking, but when we got to my office, he lingered in the doorway for a while and started talking about Diane.

"So I guess she'll live," Ray said. "It's a good thing she has such a short attention span."

"But she has the memory of an elephant," I said. I sat down in my chair, and Ray sat down too, and then I slid the copy of *Men's Times* across my desk. I just couldn't resist the opportunity to ask him for a man's opinion of Dr. Goodall's article.

"It's pretty interesting," he said. "I think she's right about some things."

"Which things?"

He shifted in his chair and held his clipboard against his chest like a little Lucite shield. "That men are driven by insecurity and low self-esteem."

"I would agree."

"But it's not intentional. I think we act out of the fog of our own confusion. It's like we spend our lives stumbling around in the dark, and sometimes we find the light switch and sometimes we don't." I raised an eyebrow, and he smiled guiltily. "And the few times someone takes us by the hand and shows us where the light switch is and even turns it on for us, it's too big of a shock. It's too wonderful and scary and unknown, and for some reason the darkness seems safer. It's what we're used to. There's no risk of getting hurt."

Just what I thought he'd say.

Bull-shit.

After lunch Joan called.

"Have you seen the *Times*?"

I hadn't. It had been a hectic morning, which had been made even more hectic by the fact that Carla had called in sick and therefore was unable to catch my overflow calls. I told Joan to hold on, and then I rummaged through a pile of mail and newspapers that had been delivered that morning and dumped on Carla's desk. I found the *Times,* went back to my office, and picked up on Joan.

"Turn to the Op-Ed page," Joan said, and when I did, I gasped. There was a huge piece by an ad hoc collective of feminists, decrying Dr. Goodall's findings as intrinsically sexist and arguing that females were just as polygamous as males.

"Fuck!" I whispered.

"Ben just came in here and told me to contact Dr. Goodall. No one's paid this much attention to this shitty magazine since . . . well . . . *ever.* He wants the next article to run earlier than June."

"Fuck!" I started to panic.

"Look. Don't panic. We'll have dinner at your place tonight and figure it out."

"But Eddie will be there."

"Fine. We'll pick his brain and see if he has any brilliant ideas."

"So what do you think?" Joan asked Eddie when we were all back at the apartment. "Are men driven by insecurity and low self-esteem? Do they act out of the fog of their own confusion?"

I had told him that she was coming over, and much to my surprise he'd offered to cook—probably to show off his dormant couple skills to someone he could possibly impress.

Eddie looked up at me and Joan and shrugged. He had just stuffed half a stick of butter into the cavity of a chicken and was now rubbing the other half over the chicken's skin. "Who wants to know?"

Joan and I exchanged glances. "We were just wondering what you thought about that piece a few weeks ago in Joan's magazine, the one by that doctor you were trying to track down for Diane."

"I liked her name," he said.

"Anything else?" Joan said, getting edgy.

"I thought it was interesting, but I think there were a few things that weren't entirely accurate."

"Like what?" Joan and I blurted at the same time.

Eddie looked at us and lit a Camel. "Like the New-Cow theory. I think there's a counterpart to that." We looked at him expectantly while he took a bong hit off his cigarette. "The New-*Bull* theory."

"Yes, we know," Joan said. "We read the Op-Ed piece too, and I'm sure there are some wild women out there, but you know as well as I do that women don't cheat anywhere as much as men do."

"I agree," I said, and Eddie looked at us.

"Well maybe not as much, but they do cheat," he said.

Joan squeezed a lime wedge into her vodka and stirred the ice with her finger. "What makes you such an expert? From what I hear you've been too busy playing the field to notice."

Eddie took a sip of Scotch. "Because Rebecca was seeing someone else."

"She was?" I asked. "While you were living together?"

"No," Eddie said, pouting like a baby. "After we split up."

"The answer is: Skinner's rats."

It was after dinner, and Joan and I had gone into the living room once Eddie had closed his door and gone to bed. When she didn't reply, I rephrased the *Jeopardy!* answer into a question.

"Why do men advance and retreat during a relationship and even after they've dumped you?" Like Ray had with me.

Joan sighed and reached for a cigarette. "To get to the other side?"

"Look, I'm sorry if I'm boring you, but this second article was *your* brilliant idea, remember?"

"You're not boring me. You never bore me. I would very much like to know the answer to that question."

"It's about evolutionary psychology," I said, then ducked in through the curtain to my room for the file and came back out.

"I can't believe you *sleep* in there," Joan said.

"Neither can I."

"Then, why don't you move? Get your own place. Take your furniture out of storage so you can have more than just a futon bed to call your own." She stopped herself. "Like I should talk. Practically all I have in my apartment is a futon bed too."

"And leave now? In the middle of my research? No way."

"Of course," Joan said. "I almost forgot."

I sat down and opened the file. "Okay, B. F. Skinner did all these experiments with rats. In one experiment he tested dispensing food to rats via a food-pellet dispenser that had a bar on it that the rats could hit to make a pellet drop down into the cage. The experiment focused on how the rats would react when the predictability with which the machine released the pellets varied."

Joan exhaled. "Continue."

"If a rat hit the bar and the food always came, the rat would quickly become bored and lose interest. It was too easy. Too predictable. *Hit the bar, food! Hit the bar, food!* It wasn't enough of a challenge."

Joan exhaled again. And began to study her split ends.

"If the rat hit the bar and the food never came, the rat would get angry and frustrated and also lose interest. It was too hopeless, too discouraging. *Hit the bar, hit the bar, hit the bar, no food! Hit the bar, hit the bar, hit the bar, no food!* The rat would get depressed and stop trying."

I reached out my fingers for a drag off Joan's cigarette before continuing. *"But,* if the food was dispensed sporadically, randomly, *unpredictably,* the rat would become frenzied. *Hit the bar, hit the bar, hit the bar, food! Hit the bar, hit the bar, hit the bar, no food! Hit the bar, hit the bar, hit the bar, still no food! Hit the bar, hit the bar, hit the bar, food food food!* The more randomly the rat was rewarded, the more obsessive it became."

Joan didn't move and didn't blink. "It's the chase thing again. Playing hard to get. They love that."

"She hates me, she hates me not."

"Why is that so damn hard to remember?"

"I know." I went back to my file.

"What? More?" Joan said.

"Gynogenetic reproduction," I said.

Joan tried to pronounce the word, but she couldn't.

"Gy-no-gen-e-tic reproduction," I repeated. *"The method of reproduction of female species that reproduce clonally using their own DNA but rely on the sperm of males from closely related species to spark the formation and development of the embryo."*

"I have no idea what you just said."

"Scientists could never understand why a male would engage in sex without the possibility of siring offspring. Producing sperm is a very big expense metabolically, and mating in general is dangerous—and males, of course, aren't exactly known for their altruism. But what they've found is that when male fish called sailfin mollies mate with the females of a related but gynogenetic species called Amazon mollies, the males become much more attractive to the females of their own species."

I paused. "You see," I continued, "the Amazon mollies look enough like female sailfin mollies to convince the female sailfins that when they see a male sailfin courting and mating with an Amazon, what they're seeing is a sailfin mating. And the females are attracted by sexually successful males. Therefore a male sailfin that bothers to help a female of another species reproduce ends up with a surplus of females for himself."

Joan stubbed out her cigarette and recrossed her legs. "Too confusing. Are you saying that Jason got involved with me for the express purpose of attracting someone else?"

"More like Ben staying with you to attract other women. Or Ray staying with Mia to attract me. Or George Costanza wearing a wedding ring. It's kind of like there's something in it for them if they appear to be domestic—if they appear to be attached to another woman."

"More sympathetic. More comfortable or experienced at being a couple."

"Right."

Joan sounded relieved, and then she sounded excited. "You had me worried for a minute there, but that's our second article."

"You think?"

"Yes, I think. And I'm going to leave now before you miss your flight back to the Institute."

RAY'S OLD-NEW COW

On the 5th of September, 1379, as two herds of swine, one belonging to the commune and the other to the priory of Saint-Marcel-le-Jeussey, were feeding together near that town, three sows of the communal herd, excited and enraged by the squealing of one of the porklings, rushed upon Perrinot Muet, the son of the swinekeeper, and before his father could come to his rescue, threw him to the ground and so severely injured him that he died soon afterwards. The three sows, after due process of law, were condemned to death; and as both the herds had hastened to the scene of the murder and by their cries and aggressive actions showed that they approved of the assault, and were ready and even eager to become *particeps criminis*, they were arrested as accomplices and sentenced by the court to suffer the same penalty.

—E. P. Evans
The Criminal Prosecution and Capital Punishment of Animals

·☾ ☽·

IF THIS WERE A SCENE in the screenplay of my life, some twenty-three-year-old studio executive would make me take it out.

"Over the top," they would have pronounced.

"Too obvious."

"Too *deus ex machina*."

"You can do better."

But I didn't make it up. It's true. And it would definitely be restored in the director's cut.

It really happened.

And because it really happened, it became, as we embittered loser monkey scientists like to say, *material*.

The day I'm referring to is the day that I saw Evelyn walking down the hall at work wearing Ray's shirt.

The light-blue-and-white-striped long-sleeved T-shirt.

The one I had bought for him on a warm Sunday afternoon in late August the weekend after we'd seen the apartment in Chelsea.

It was just about a week after my second article had appeared, and I was finally starting to enjoy the media buzz it had generated. That Friday morning I had awoken with an unusual amount of vim and vigor, and I had raced to the office propelled by the private and premature self-congratulatory belief that my homegrown form of therapy seemed to be working:

I, Dr. Marie Goodall, was a Nobel-Prize-worthy genius. Maybe Larry King would agree to interview me in disguise. Or, better yet, Barbara Walters.

That's when I saw the shirt.

I will never forget standing there in the hall watching Evelyn walk toward me in that shirt, and how I nodded good morning to her as if nothing were wrong, and how I made myself start walking again before she noticed that my insides were caving in. Whatever progress I had made drained out of me suddenly and completely.

She was wearing his shirt.

I couldn't think about the rest of it yet.

I sat down at my desk.

My hands were shaking.

Adrenaline was coursing through my body at lightning speed, and I was afraid I might faint or that my heart would explode. I stood up and shut my door, and then I sat back down at my desk and stared at the phone.

An hour later I picked up the receiver.

And dialed Ray's extension.

We made small talk for a minute or two, and then somehow I think I finally said, *Evelyn is wearing your shirt. The shirt I gave you,* and he said, *I know,* and then I said, *Are you two seeing each other?* and he said, *Yes, I guess we are.*

We were silent. *How long have you known?* he said, and then, to save face, even though by that point I didn't have much of it left to save, I said, *For a while I guess, but I was never really sure.*

So, do you hate me? he asked, and I said, *I don't know, I don't think so,* and then he said, *I'm glad. I would hate it if you hated me.*

He made a joke then, or maybe I made one, I'm not sure which now, and sometime after that we hung up. I remember staring at the phone and watching it ring a little while later though I couldn't hear it, and that Carla came to my door and told me Joan was holding.

I watched my hand pick up the receiver, and then I felt my lips moving as I told Joan what had happened.

"Jesus," she said.

"I feel like I'm going to throw up. Like I'm . . . Like everything is . . ." I had no idea how to finish the sentence, so I didn't.

"Jesus," Joan said again. "What are you going to do?"

The nausea passed, but a deep, crushing feeling that I was rapidly losing ground—that I was regressing and that a major setback was imminent—replaced it. "I don't know," I said. "I can't talk right now."

"Listen to me. Don't do anything stupid, okay?"

I was silent.

"Jane? I'll call you later at home. Okay?"

"Okay," I said finally, and hung up.

Then I closed my door and proceeded to smoke myself through the next six hours.

At the end of the day, after everyone had cleared out for their summer beach weekends, Eddie stuck his head in my doorway.

"Are you ready to leave?"

I looked up at him. "Leave?" I thought for a second or two. "No, actually. I have a few things to finish up. I'll see you at home later."

"I probably won't be there."

I said nothing.

"Are you okay?" Eddie asked.

"Yes, I'm fine."

"You look . . ."

"I'm just tired," I said. "Long day. Long week." I lit a cigarette and started shuffling papers around on my desk. "I'll see you later."

After an hour I went into Ray's office and ransacked his desk, went through his drawers, through all his papers, and when I found no traces of Evelyn, I ransacked Evelyn's desk.

Did I say *setback*? This was more like a psychotic break.

And there, in the back of her top drawer, where she kept pencils and pens and loose change, I found her date book from the past year. I took the date book back to my office and shut the door, and then I sat down and flipped through the pages, back to the fall before the January that Ray and I had met:

September.

October.

November.

Haircut.

Gym.

Parents in town.

December.

January.

February.

Dentist.

Chiropractor.

Ballet.

March.

April.

May.

Dinner with R.

Bike ride with R.

Movie with R.

June.

Dinner with R.

Central Park with R.

Mercer St.

I felt my mouth drop open. They *had* been seeing each other before us—*right* before us, I realized. *Right up until the night before the hair imitation.*

I continued flipping the pages:

July through October (while Ray and I were seeing each other and right after we stopped).

Nothing.

November.

December.

Nothing.

January.

Weekend at R's parents.

February.

March.

April.

Picnic.

Yale w/R for reunion.

Weekend in Montauk.

They had been seeing each other all year—*all year, those motherfuckers!*—going to movies and reunions and fucking *Montauk* while I had been moping around Eddie's apartment, with my different kinds of sadness, reading all those fucking books on monkeys!

But it didn't make sense.

Evelyn wasn't a *New* Cow: She was technically an *Old* Cow. Like Mia.

Like me.

Only he had stayed with Mia and gone back to Evelyn.

*Un*like me.

I couldn't think about that now—the idea that the New-Cow theory was *invalid*—so I xeroxed the relevant pages of Evelyn's date book, returned the date book to her desk, grabbed a few accordion files from the supply cabinet on my way out, and went home, still boiling.

I emerged from the subway downtown and stopped at a liquor store around the corner from the apartment to pick up a pint of Jack Daniel's. I opened the bottle and took several gulps from it before I'd even gotten home, and then, once inside, I continued to swig from it as I paced from the living room through the hole in my wall and back out again, trying to figure out what to do next.

I got my notebook.

MOTHERFUCKER! I wrote in big block permanent-black demented letters, like that inscription to Eddie in the commitmentphobia book, and recounted the day's events in increasingly illegible handwriting. Joan called several times while I was writing, leaving frantic messages on the machine wanting to know how I was and where I was, but I didn't pick up the phone. I couldn't talk yet. All I could do was drink and pace and write, trying to fit the smooth little pieces of the scenario back together: whether Ray had left me for Evelyn or had just started seeing her afterward because he was lonely; whether they'd been seeing each other for a while or it had started recently—and what the deal was with Mia. Whatever the correct scenario was, I couldn't get over the fact that not only were they sleeping together but I, Dr. Marie Goodall, had not known.

But the most devastating part of it was that my research had obscured the biggest truth of all: that Ray had moved on—to someone else—and I had not.

I went into my room and picked up the manila envelope off the floor and dumped its contents onto the bed. Papers, photographs, poems, stupid little seaside souvenirs Ray had given me fell onto the blanket. For a minute I was tempted to throw it all out the window into the alley.

But I didn't.

I wouldn't.

It was evidence: evidence that our relationship had existed; evidence that I hadn't been crazy—at least not then.

I opened one accordion file and put all the papers and photographs neatly into it and marked the front "EVIDENCE" in big black letters. Then I went to my desk and took all my notes—all my scraps of paper, all the xeroxed pages from books, all the newspaper and magazines articles, the list of Eddie's girlfriends, all my notebooks and case files, and the pages I'd copied from Evelyn's date book, and put them into two other accordion files marked "PROOF."

I stared at the accordion folders.

Then I grabbed a yellow legal pad from my desk.

Like a drunk, determined "F. U." Bailey, I addressed myself to the task of assessing damages with surprising clearheadedness, given my elevated blood alcohol level. And then I passed out.

JANE GOODALL V. RAY BROWN
Settlement Suit in Favor of Plaintiff
Defendant Ordered to Pay the Following Damages

Compensatory Damages:

To compensate for expenses incurred as a direct result of emotional and psychic injury:

Liquor:
    1 pint Jack Daniel's sour mash bourbon per week @ $7.50 per pint   390.00

Self-help books:
    10 @ $22.50   229.50

Research materials (books, magazines, notebooks, etc.) 210.50

Cigarettes:
    1 pack per day @ $2.25 per pack   821.25

Kleenex:
    1 box per week @ $1.25 per box   65.00

Häagen-Dazs:
    3 pints per week @ $2.69 per pint   419.64

Agnes B. *hommes* striped T-shirt   98.00

Reupholstery for what-will-become-of-me couch   600.00
                           ———————

                Total Compensatory Damages: $2833.89

Punitive Damages:

To punish defendant for inflicting excessive and undue emotional damage on plaintiff and to deter defendant from repeating injurious behavior:

                           $1,225,500.00

Hedonic Damages:

Compensation for loss of quality of life and self-esteem, hopeful outlook on future, personal happiness, and missed social-interaction opportunities:

$1000 per day $ 365,000.00

                   TOTAL DAMAGES $1,593,333.89

THE MORNING AFTER

Man has places in his heart which do not yet exist, and into them enters suffering in order that they may have existence.

—Léon Bloy, 1846–1917

·☾ ☽·

Two blurred figures—a man and a woman—cross a charming room: cozy, warm, with red-velvet walls and a fire burning in the fireplace. Voices are heard, as is a persistent heartbeat: Flub-dub. Flub-dub. Flub-dub.

"God. This apartment is great! It's huge!" the man says.

"I know," says the woman. "How did you hear about it?"

The man scratches his head. "I don't know really. I've never been on this street, let alone seen this building, but it's as if somehow I sensed it was here."

They proceed through the vast, fabulous apartment, discussing furnishings and how they will decorate it. They kiss, hold hands, and move into the bedroom.

Flub-dub. Flub-dub. Flub-dub.

"Now that we actually have a bedroom, I think we should buy a bed," the man says. "A real one, with a headboard and a footboard. One that's not directly on the floor."

The woman sighs, obviously moved with emotion. "A bed of our own. That we've slept in only with each other. God. I can't believe this is happening."

The man sighs, obviously moved too. "Me either. I've never felt this way about anyone before. It's as if some kind of destiny has brought us together, and brought us here. I love you, Evelyn."

"I love you too, Ray."

Flub-dub.

[POST-NIGHTMARE SCREAM DELETED.]

I woke up late the next morning, my head aching from a hangover, my heart pounding from the dream. I felt numb with sadness and misery and crankiness.

After I showered and made coffee, I went into the living room with my cup and sat down at the table to smoke and think. I desperately needed to figure out what to do with my anger so I wouldn't kill anyone.

Old Cows who discover New Cows are fit to be tied.

I was on my second cup of coffee and my third cigarette when Eddie got up and came out of his bedroom. He'd been out very late the night before with friends from out of town. I wasn't looking forward to telling him about my mind-altering discovery. The humiliation and the embarrassment would be too much; I didn't think I could take any more of either.

He tied the belt of his robe and smiled at me, still warm and fuzzy from sleep.

I shifted my gaze out the window. He walked over to the table, took a sip from my coffee cup, pulled a cigarette out of the pack and lit it.

"What's the matter with you?"

I stared at him again. "Ray's fucking Evelyn."

Why beat around the bush, right?

Eddie raised an eyebrow. "How'd you find out?"

"She wore his shirt to work yesterday. A shirt I bought him."

He looked at the lit end of his cigarette and sat down at the table across from me. "I'm sorry," he said.

I nodded, completely unconsoled. "Thanks."

"Were you surprised?" he said.

I waited a beat to make sure I'd heard his question correctly. "Ex*cuse* me?"

He shrugged. "I'm not. They spend a lot of time together. I

mean, look, he's attractive, she's attractive, they're healthy normal people of the opposite sex. It's just not that big a leap to make, that's all."

I didn't take my eyes off his face. He knew something I didn't. "Don't tell me—"

"What?"

"Don't tell me you knew."

"No. I didn't know. But I suspected."

"You *suspec*ted? Why didn't you tell me?"

"Jane, they're always together at the office. They go to work parties together. I've seen them eat off each other's plates. And, when I go over to Evelyn's desk to shoot the shit, Ray always seems to appear, as if to reclaim his territory." He paused. "I assumed you wondered about them too but just didn't want to know."

I felt like the biggest idiot in the world. While I had wondered, I had never gone further than that—not because the idea had never crossed my mind that they could be involved but because I'd never sensed any spark whatsoever between them. They seemed like, you know, *friends*.

"Well, I know it's hard for you to comprehend, but not everyone fucks everything in sight just because it's there."

"At least I fuck," he said.

"And so would I if there were someone halfway decent around to fuck *with*."

Eddie's mouth dropped open, and he started to laugh, and despite myself I laughed too. But the humor of that exchange passed quickly.

"I'm worried about you," Eddie said.

I glared at him. "Why?"

"You're letting this thing consume your life. You have to get over it."

"Oh, I'll get over it," I said, reeling with hunger to start plotting and planning anew. "I assure you, I'll get over it."

"How?"

I got up from the table and headed off toward my hole.

"Where are you going?" Eddie said.

"Out," I said, slamming the curtain.

Before I left the apartment, I called Joan and told her to meet me at the Bull and Bear at the Waldorf for Bloody Marys. I took the subway uptown and arrived there first, then sat down at a table by the window and ordered a mineral water with ice and lime. Outside, Lexington Avenue was empty. But the Bull and Bear wasn't. As usual on summer weekends in New York when the city emptied out of natives, only tourists and lonely people wandered the streets and sat in bars to escape the heat.

Joan arrived sweating, her hair afrizz.

"You look terrible," she said, and wiped her face with the napkin.

"You should talk."

"I know. There has to be a cure for our hair." She sat down and signaled the waiter. "What, no booze?" she said, pointing to my glass. "Or is that straight gin?"

"No booze," I repeated calmly and seriously. "I need to be clearheaded and sharp. I need to have my wits about me."

Joan ordered a Bloody Mary. "For what?"

I smiled my best psycho-smile.

Old Cows take bovine-icide extremely seriously.

"Nothing will make me feel better unless he dies a slow and painful death." I squeezed the lime wedge into my mineral water and stirred the ice cubes with my finger.

Joan looked at me. There was a momentary flash of concern

in her eyes, but it seemed to pass. She knew what it was like to feel this way.

"Where does he even get the time to fool around so much? I mean, he's still living with Mia." I shook my head. "I guess Evelyn's sweet and stupid enough to swallow that brother-sister bullshit whole."

"Youth," Joan said.

We stared at each other.

"I want him to die," I pronounced.

"Yes, I know."

"No, I mean, I want to bury him in print." I took one of Joan's Marlboros and lit it.

She sipped her Bloody Mary and lit a cigarette too. "You mean, like, writing another piece?"

I grinned. "Only this time I want to get specific. Really specific. Like, do a case study on him—an ultraspecific case study. I'm going to fucking nail him to the wall this time."

Joan seemed afraid to interrupt me. She didn't say anything and waited for me to continue.

I pulled a book out of my bag—*Sexual Selection: Mate Choice and Courtship in Nature* (Gould & Gould, 1989)—and opened it to a chapter I'd marked. "You see, there are three kinds of monogamy. Permanent monogamy is a pair-bond that lasts until the death of one member."

"Yeah, right."

"Serial monogamy," I continued, "is when a pair rears its offspring together but then immediately finds new mates." I flipped the page. "And then there's annual monogamy, when a pair stays together through one breeding season but then finds new partners the next year."

"Like . . . Ray and you?" Joan asked tentatively.

I snorted. "Except for the fact that I didn't find a new part-ner, and he didn't even wait a whole year." I put the book back in my bag and leaned across the table. "You see, my idea is to tailor the concept of annual monogamy to fit Ray. I'd propose the notion of semiannual monogamy and back it up with his case history." I sipped my water and felt cleansed and heady with purpose. "Of course, I'd change his name and all that other bullshit for the magazine."

Joan nodded slowly. "I'll take it to Ben once you've done a draft, and if he approves it, I'll try to figure out how to get it in as soon as possible." She pulled out her date book and made a few notes. "When do you think you'll get started on it?"

I signaled the waiter for the check. "Now."

I spent the week writing the article, and by the following Monday morning Joan had it on her desk. She brought it into her editorial meeting for review, and by three o'clock Tuesday afternoon she called to tell me that it had been approved but that because of a summer double-issue and various other space constraints, the earliest it could run would be October. On stands: September 21.

A year, almost exactly, from my last mate with Ray.

That night I sat on the what-will-become-of-me couch, feeling drained and exhausted from finishing the column and all that had precipitated it. But I was also exhilarated at the notion that revenge was finally in sight. I leaned my head back, closed my eyes, and breathed a heavy sigh of relief. Which was when Eddie came home.

I heard him pour himself a drink in the kitchen, then walk slowly down the narrow hallway to the living room. He smiled at me, then sat down at the table with a copy of the previous month's *Men's Times* article. Apparently he had a different term for the male sailfin's behavior described therein.

"Off-ramp," he said.

His feet were up on the table, and he was noisily chewing two pieces of Nicorette at the same time. He was trying to give up cigarettes because Denise, his latest teenage girlfriend, had just told him she wanted to marry someone who smoked.

I looked up. "What?"

Eddie took his feet off the table and reached over to the magazine and pointed to a paragraph on the second page.

"Why males participate in gy-ro-genetic reproduction, or whatever the fuck it's called," he said. "I think it's because they're using the new female as an off-ramp from the other female."

I rolled my eyes. "First of all, it's *gyno,* not *gyro.* And second of all, the whole point of the other *useless* female is to lure the *new* female."

Eddie stared at me. "Well, maybe it's both."

I stared back.

"Take Stephanie," he said, "the girlfriend whose name you didn't bother to learn. I knew I wanted to break up with her, and as soon as I did, I simultaneously knew I needed a good reason to do it: another girlfriend. By getting involved with Denise, I was able to leave Stephanie, and because of my 'sadness' over leaving Stephanie, I was able to get involved with Denise more quickly and more deeply."

"Wait a minute, wait a minute, *wait a minute!*" I put my fingers to my temples and pressed as hard as I could. "Is that really true? Is that how you really think? That women are fucking *off-ramps*?"

Eddie looked up at the ceiling and chewed his gum faster.

"Not consciously, no. In fact, it just kind of came to me now, as I was saying it." He looked rather pleased with himself. Then he threw his head back and laughed maniacally.

I sat up straighter and looked at Eddie suspiciously. "What's so funny?" I asked.

He crossed one leg over the other and swung his foot back and forth. "Don't worry. Your secret is safe with me."

"What's that supposed to mean?"

"It means, I'm *on* to you and Joan. I know about 'Dr. Goodall.' "

My heart was racing. I looked over at the magazine on the table and then over at the television, which I wished were on. "I don't know what you're talking about."

He threw his head back and laughed again. "Oh, come on! I heard you two in the living room that night. You thought I was asleep, but I could hear you, plotting away." He reached across the table and took a cigarette out of my pack and lit it. *"Hit the bar, hit the bar, hit the bar, food!"* he said, pawing the table as if it might dispense a food pellet.

I closed my eyes and took a deep breath. Then I turned back toward Eddie.

"If you ever open your fat fucking mouth to anyone about this, I will personally take out an ad in *The New York Times* and tell everyone what an unbelievable slut you are, and then I'll plaster copies of your *love letter* all over the office."

Eddie took a drag off his cigarette and stopped chewing. "What love letter?"

I looked at him and smiled maliciously. "The love letter you wrote to the daughter of a famous network news anchor and were stupid enough to leave in the magazine rack in the bathroom. You met her for two seconds at some party, and then you wrote her a fucking love letter telling her how *entrancing* she was! And you couldn't even *spell* the fucking word! You spelled it with an s—*entransing!*"

Eddie doubled over and laughed so hard his Nicorette fell out of his mouth.

I was laughing now too. "You know, there's a clinical term for people like you, people who think they're involved with someone even though the object of their affection doesn't even know who they are: *Erotomaniacs.* Your *entransing* wife. *In your fucking dreams!*"

When we finally stopped laughing, we both sat up and wiped our eyes. Eddie lit another cigarette and broke open a fresh piece of Nicorette.

"Don't worry, Jane. I won't tell. Why would I want anyone knowing that I live with a sixty-five-year-old woman? It would ruin my reputation."

"What's left of it."

He wiped his eyes again and put the gum in his mouth. "But seriously, Jane."

"Seriously what?"

"I think you've gone far enough."

"What's that supposed to mean?"

"I mean," he started slowly, "that I saw the draft of your third article. The one about semiannual monogamy."

I felt my face turn bright red with rage. "How do you know about that?"

Eddie chewed his gum nervously. "I saw it. In your room."

"You went into my room and went through my *files?*"

"It was on your desk."

"*Bull*shit," I yelled. "It was not on my desk. It was in a file."

Eddie stopped chewing. "Okay. It was in a file."

I stared at him, incredulous. "How could you *do* that?"

He shrugged, and shook his foot nervously. "I was worried

about you," he said. "Ever since you found out about Ray and Evelyn, you've been acting like a stalker. Look, you made your point already. The first two pieces were great. Interesting. Funny. Clever. Even *I* learned something. But you're taking this column thing a little too seriously."

"So? That's my business."

"Well, it's my business too. We're roommates." He paused. "We're friends."

"No, we're not," I said. "We're not *friends*. We're acquaintances. Partners in misery. Drinking buddies. You never gave me the time of day before I moved in here, and I can assure you, you won't give me the time of day as soon as I move out—which I promise you will be very soon."

"Jesus, you'd better get a grip."

"*I'd* better get a grip? What about *you*? Talk about stalking. How many years did you pine over *your* beloved? Not to mention the number of replacements you've gone through and the speed at which you dispose of them. Don't tell *me* to get a grip when there aren't enough women in this city to fill the hole you think she left. The only reason this situation worked is because we needed each other. You needed someone to absorb your narcissism, and I needed a subject."

He stared at me, and I was shocked to see that he looked wounded by what I'd just said.

"Is that what you think this has been? A *research* arrangement?"

I didn't say anything. I don't know what I thought. Nothing had made any sense since the night Ray dumped me.

He shook his head slowly. "Jane. It's over with Ray."

"Over?" I stared at him. "*Over?* It's not fucking over. It's not over this time until *I* say it's over."

"Why can't you just accept the fact that he's an asshole and move on?"

"Because," I said. "Because I can't."

"Because why?"

I stared at him and bit my lip to keep the tears from coming. "Because. I still love him. Because I never felt that way about anyone in my whole life."

"And someday you'll feel that way about someone else."

I shook my head and bit my lip harder, but the tears escaped out of the corners of my eyes and down my cheeks. "No. I won't."

"Yes. You will."

"No. I won't."

"Jane. He's not the last man you're ever going to love."

I stared at him, and he stared back. Then he sat down next to me on the couch.

"He's not the last man who will ever love *you*."

I squeezed my eyes shut and covered them with my hand. The tears were unstoppable now.

"Yes, he is," I whispered.

"No, he's not."

I sobbed into my hands and felt like I would never be able to stop.

"No, he's not," Eddie said again. Then he put his arms around me. "I swear, he's not."

ANIMAL HUSBANDRY

husband *n* 1: a married man, esp. when considered in relation to his wife 2: *Brit:* a manager 3: *archaic:* a prudent or frugal manager—*vt* 1: to manage, esp. with prudent economy 2: to use frugally; to conserve: to husband one's resources 3: *archaic* a: to be or become a husband to; to marry b: to find a husband for c: to till; cultivate [bef. 1000; ME *husband(e)*, OE *husbonda* master of the house]
husbandry *n* 1: the cultivation and production of edible crops or of animals for food; agriculture; farming 2: the science of raising crops or food animals 3: careful or thrifty management; frugality, thrift, or conservation 4: the management of domestic affairs or of resources generally [1250–1300; ME *housebondrie*]

·《 》·

WELL, I'M SORRY TO SAY that there's no big surprise ending here.

No fabulous nite of luv with Eddie.

No running off to Tanzania to join up with the real Jane Goodall to analyze primate fecal trails for the rest of my life.

No, the only surprise was that after all was said and done, after all my theories and conclusions about men in general and men in particular had been formulated, it was Eddie—Eddie the womanizer, Eddie the heartbreaker, Eddie the *animal* who refused to give up on the idea that his perfect mate was out there somewhere—who brought me to an understanding that flew in the face of everything I wanted to believe was true. And it was Eddie who led me through the tunnel of sadness and pointed out the pin dot of light a few hundred thousand yards away.

I still believe in things like allelomimetic behavior and gynogenetic reproduction and semiannual monogamy, but if I believe in these things, I have to believe in permanent monogamy too, right?

Sometimes a monkey is just a monkey.

And sometimes a guy is just being a guy.

But other times, well, let's just say, even monkeys hold a few surprises in store for the watchful monkey scientist.

Okay. Let's get back to the couch when the dam broke, when the misery and rage and dementia and scientific obsession fell away, and all that was left was what I'd used every ounce of will trying to avoid in the first place:

Grief.

Loss.

And sadness.

And when the sobs reduced themselves to hiccups, Eddie gave me a drink, poured himself one, and tried to get me to laugh by telling me an all-new new-wife story. Then he turned on the TV, and I fell asleep beside him as he watched the last third of *Rooster Cogburn and the Lady* (any John Wayne movie was better than no John Wayne movie at all). And when I woke up the next morning, Eddie was still there. Fully clothed. Mouth slightly open. Snoring lightly.

I rubbed my stiff neck and went to the kitchen to put on a pot of coffee. Then I called Joan and told her that Dr. Marie Goodall had died peacefully in her sleep.

It was time to get on with my life.

So where's everybody now?

David fell in love with a jet-setting photographer on the West Coast who regularly transfers frequent flier miles into his account.

Joan got a great offer for a job at *Newsweek*—science editor if you can believe it. When she told Ben and he didn't make a counteroffer, she took it as a sign—a big neon sign—to move on, too.

Ray was hired to executive-produce a fledgling network news magazine show. Evelyn stayed behind to torture me.

But I got Ray's job.

And Eddie works for me now. He has yet to track down Kevin Costner, but he's perpetually hot on the trail of a new wife.

———

Instead of destroying the case files, I buried them in a moldy storage bin in the basement of my new prewar doorman apartment building on the Upper East Side.

I'm still a sucker for New World monkeys, the *New York Times'* science section, and an Old Cow's Old-Cow story.

I still read Ray's horoscope when I read my own.

And every once in a while I still dream about him. But the dream is different now, and I am different in it.

In the dream I see him in a place that seems familiar but isn't: on a beach we never went to; across a crowded room of strangers; in a field as barren and devoid of features as a moonscape.

Our eyes lock.

And there, in the soundless, gravityless atmosphere of that place, the place where memory and experience and love and grief meet to form acceptance—the place where Old Cows and New Cows don't exist—I turn away and whisper words I thought would never come:

Moo who?

Acknowledgments

I am grateful beyond expression to the following people for years of extraordinary friendship: Marian Brown, Julie Grau, Ivan Held, Wendy Law-Yone, Jennifer Loviglio, Tom Perry, and Daren Salter. Nowhere in the world are there wiser, funnier, or more generous friends than these.

Or these: Paul Bogaards, Ruth Fecych, Kate Fitzgerald, Dalma Heyn, Martha Johnson, Julie Just, Nina King, Linda Lehrer, David Leibowitz, Julia Matheson, Francie Norris, Chuck O'Connor, Nancy Pearlstein, John Scardino, Peter J. Smith, Nicky Weinstock, Carl Wagner, and Sonnie Willson.

Special thanks to: Marty Arnold, Steven Barclay, Damon Boone, George and Laurie Bower, Stephanie Bower, Anna Caraveli, Elizabeth Chandler, Charles Goff, Lynn Goldberg, Paul Hallam, John Harris, Paul Hartman, Howard and Stella Heffron, Barbara Jackson, Debbie Kautzman, the staff at the Kennedy-Warren, Richard Kosoff, Nicole Kosoff, Bob Lemstrom-Sheedy, Binney Levine, Lorraine and Michael Loviglio, Margaret Maupin, Anton Mueller, Lynda Obst, Relish, Greg Riley, Billy Shore, and Tom Spanbauer. I am very grateful to Bret Easton Ellis for reading an early draft and helping to redirect me, and to Edmund White for reading, too, and for his encouragement when I most needed it. I also wish to thank my rotating team of physicians for their various expertises: Dr. Richard Firshein, Dr. Robert Heffron, Dr. Howard Hoffman, and especially Denise Zalman, C.S.W.

For expert representation, endless hilarity, and unflagging loyalty in matters both professional and personal, I wish to thank

Bill Clegg. I also wish to thank Kathy Robbins for her sage advice and the rest of the fabulous staff at The Robbins Office: Kate Alvarez, Eric Chinski, Judith Greenberg, David Halpern, Kevin Lang, Elizabeth Oldroyd, Tifany Richards, Robert Simpson, and Cory Wickwire. In addition, the brilliant minds of Rick Pappas and CAA's Robert Bookman deserve special mention.

For her herculean editing efforts, undivided attention, and friendship, I am grateful to my editor, Susan Kamil. Every author should be so lucky. Carla Riccio's editorial suggestions were equally invaluable, as were those of Julie Grau. I am also indebted to many others at The Dial Press and BDD, including: Stuart Applebaum, Carole Baron, Leslie Hermsdorf, Libby Jordan, Gretchen Koss, Laura Rossi, Cary Ryan, Leslie Schnur, Linda Steinman, and publicity oxen Carisa Hays and Tracy Locke. Not to mention Michael Ian Kaye, Barbara DeWilde, and Francesca Belanger for their artistic talents.

Lastly, I wish to thank my friend Charmaine Re, who discovered the Old-Cow–New-Cow theory. Without it, clearly, this book could never have been written.

Also coming soon from Laura Zigman,
her latest, sharply witty novel,

DATING BIG BIRD

DATING BIG BIRD

IT'S NOT THAT I found Big Bird particularly attractive, it's just that I thought he would make a good father.

Parent, Marian would correct me. *Father* implied an extended relationship with the mother we were not necessarily banking on.

Not that we wouldn't have wanted an extended relationship. It's just that we were trying to be realistic. We were thirty-three, after all, and by then we knew the difference between expectation and desire; between love and lust; between boyfriends and potential husbands and fathers—I mean, parents.

At least, we were supposed to know.

Contemplating impregnation by an eight-foot yellow bird is just one example of how carried away you can get when you want children as much as we did.

You have to admit, though, that except for the feathers—and the horizontally-striped tights, and the bulging eyes, and that stupid pointy beak—Big Bird would be the ideal parent.

He's warm.

He's affectionate.

He's had a stable job for almost as long as I can remember.

And you'd always know where to find him in case you needed anything later on.

Giving birth to a baby covered in a fuzzy down of yellow

feathers would be a small price to pay for such exemplary paternal qualities.

Marian, though, preferred Barney. She would cite his trademark song as evidence of his superior genes.

♫ *I love you. You love me. We're a happy family . . .* ♫

But when I'd remind her of the inconsistency of her argument—how a happy family might be beyond our reach but a child wasn't—she'd agree.

Then she'd confess the true reason for her preference:

She liked purple better than yellow.

I did not always want to have a child.

It came to me relatively late in life, compared to some of my friends who knew they wanted children at about the same time they decided which college to go to.

With me, it took longer.

It took until I grew tired of myself and wished for the relief of distraction.

It took until the nights became too quiet and too lonely to bear.

It took until I laid eyes on my niece.

That's when I knew I just had to have one.

And when I knew there was no going back.

Obviously, I understood that I would need to prepare for such a radical addition to my life—to feather my nest, as it were.

First, I would need a bigger apartment to make room for a crib.

And a changing table.

And a Diaper Genie.

Two, I would need the crib. And the changing table. And the Diaper Genie.

Three, I would need more money. So I could afford the bigger apartment. And the nursery equipment. Not to mention the nanny, since I would have to keep working to pay for it all.

"Aren't you forgetting something?" Marian would ask.

I'd stare at her blankly.

Crib.

Changing table.

Diaper Genie.

Bigger apartment.

Better job.

Nanny.

And then it would dawn on me. "Stroller."

"I see," she'd say, giggling and slapping her leg. "So you're still planning on reproducing asexually."

For a while, actually, I wasn't planning on reproducing at all. I thought I might just kidnap my niece and spare myself all the trouble and aggravation.

Why risk having a child you might not like when there's already an existing child you adore?

At first, my sister was moved by such displays of my passionate aunt-hood. Then, as the first year passed and moved into the second, and Nicole, The Pickle, became more and more of an animal, she began to really latch on to the idea.

"You can have her," she'd say, staring at the floor where the screeching wailing flailing fit-throwing beast-in-a-diaper had thrown herself down in protest over an enforced nap.

But each display of histrionics only made me covet her more.

She's an animal, I'd swoon. *But she's my animal*.

Not that I really considered stealing her.

I wasn't *that* demented.

I just liked to borrow her sometimes. Take the baby-idea out for a little reality test-drive.

Pushing the stroller through the park, taking her for a ride in the family Jeep, dragging her kicking and screaming through the supermarket when she should have been eating or napping, I'd beam at passers-by with the imagined pride and bliss of a new mother.

"She's got her father's temperament," I'd say, and shrug blamelessly.

Which was true.

My brother-in-law always gets cranky when he's hungry and tired.

Telling people you want to get pregnant when you're not married doesn't exactly go over like The Red Balloon. I mean, it's not like everyone you know—parents, boyfriends, single friends, married friends—will be waiting in a receiving line to embrace you and congratulate you on having a few too many vodka martinis and transforming yourself, on cue, into the living breathing Female Cliché.

I want to have a bay-bay, you slur those times when the urge simply overtakes you—your lower lip sagging to reveal a river of drool just waiting to drip down your chin; your face contorting into the picture of the pathetic lonely unfulfilled single woman they just know, deep down, you are.

But, for once, you are not feeling particularly pathetic.

For once, you are not bemoaning your unmarried barren state.

Despite the fact that you are, quite obviously, drunk, you're in surprisingly good spirits.

In fact, you're feeling rather empowered.

Giving voice to your desire to have a child is the first step to achieving it.

If there were one thing I could do besides have a baby, it would be this:

To eradicate from the face of the earth all traces of the phrase *biological clock*.

I hate this phrase. Not only is it annoyingly overused and pejorative, but it is stupid and incorrect.

Late at night, when I lie awake in the dark, wondering how I got to wherever it is I've gotten to, the image of a huge Big Ben clock ticking away my child-bearing years is not the first one that comes to mind.

At least, not to my mind, anyway.

This is what comes to my mind:

A gum-ball machine.

Dispensing its limited supply of eggs.

One by one.

Month after month.

Year after year.

Egg.

Egg.

Egg.

The weekend I ran into Marian after not seeing her since high school was not a good weekend.

A close friend of mine had come to New York for a big fancy wedding at the Waldorf, and I had offered to babysit her four-year-old son Nicholas on Saturday night in their hotel room so she and her husband could enjoy the nuptial festivities downstairs.

After we'd ordered up room service, and watched several hours of Barney video tapes, and played *Chutes and Ladders*, he climbed up on to my lap as I read him *Curious George*. Sitting there as I turned the pages, he suddenly became interested in the ring I wore on my right hand—gold, with a big almost-clear light green stone in it (merely decorative)— than in the plot of the story.

"Where your hud-band?" he asked, staring at the ring.

I smiled. "I don't have a *hud*-band," I replied without shame and with just enough lilt in my voice to even suggest pride.

"Do you have a big boy?"

A big boy? "You mean, a boyfriend?"

He nodded.

"No." Less pride. A little more shame.

His forehead grew furrowed. "Do you have a baby?"

Ditto my forehead. "No."

"Do you have . . . a dog?"

"No."

"Do you have . . . a cat?"

"No."

Deeper furrows. "Do you have . . . a giraffe?"

"No."

"Do you have . . . an elephant?"

"No."

He scanned the room, desperate to find something in it I might possibly have. Finally, he spied a small bouquet of flowers on the dresser. "Do you have flowers?"

"No."

He stared at me, then shrugged his shoulders with his arms outstretched at his sides. "Then *what* do you *have?*"

I have nothing.

Nothing, that is, except for a big job working for a big designer.

The job?

Director of Public Relations, Karen Lipps New York.

The designer?

Five-foot-ten.

One-hundred and seventy-two pounds.

Easily a size sixteen if she weren't a clothing designer and couldn't sew her own size six labels into whatever she wore.

Karen Lipps was only ten years older than me, but she had a multi-gazillion dollar company that had just gone public; four houses and another under contract; and a little girl, aged three.

The latter of which was why she wasn't as thin as she used to be.

"She's not as thin as she used to be, ever since she had . . . *the child,*" her fawning but slightly evil British Uriah Heep-like assistant, Simon Queen, once whispered to me upon exiting a meeting. Karen had been particularly harsh about a pant sample that made the model look like she'd actually eaten in the past three weeks and she had thrown a peeled banana at Annette, who oversaw the sample seamstresses. Whenever Karen threw food at someone, Simon felt responsibility—and perhaps his one opportunity to get a word in edgewise all day—to deconstruct her pathology to anyone who would listen.

"It drives her absolutely mad when the clothes don't lie completely flat against the body or if there's the slightest bit of puckering," he continued in his hushed tone. "She considers it an injustice: *the illusion of fat where there really isn't any*." He paused then, and tucked his straight chin-length hair neatly behind his ears. "She hates fat, you see. Because she hates *being* fat. Not that she'd ever admit to it, poor thing. In her mind, she's still a size four."

"Try telling her pants that."

"Believe me, I've tried," he said and lit a Dunhill. "But Lycra will only stretch so far."

I actually knew her back when she was still a size four.

Back when her name wasn't plastered on billboards and buses and full-page newspaper ads and sneakers and baseball caps and perfume bottles and underwear.

Back when her name was still Karen Lipsky.

Seven years ago, she had just gone out on her own after ten years with a top female designer and I was a junior copywriter at the ad agency she had hired to position herself in the market. At the time, I was only slightly ambivalent about my job since I was hard at work in my spare time on a collection of tragi-comic short stories about my loser life in the opposed to now, when I am completely repulsed only about who I can possibly beg to sleep a baby), and so one day, during one of etings she insisted on attending at parent reason, with the idea that she should change her name.

"Change my *name?*" she said, her malnourished bony twist of a body turning in her swivel chair to face me. She bit her big lipsticked lips and stared at me over the plume of smoke coming out of her nose. "What do you mean, *change my name?*"

I had no idea what I meant. What I *did* know was that she needed to have a corporate identity ready before the fall buying season began and all we had so far was *LipskyLook.* With that we'd be lucky if J.C. Penney took her.

"Maybe the name of your line should relate more to your design philosophy," I heard myself pontificate. "Maybe the name will help connect the wearer to the clothes."

She was still biting her lips, but she hadn't yelled at me yet. Which I took as a sign to continue.

"A name," I said slowly, gathering all of my bullshitting skills in one glorious breath—*I was a writer, after all, with layers and layers of creative talent that were, as yet, untapped!*— "that describes the woman who will wear your clothes. A name that evokes style. Urbanity. Sophistication. Sex." I came up for air and to buy myself another crucial few seconds of time, and when I did, I noticed her mouth—licked clean of her signature mud matte pigment, and ravenous for success.

"Lipps," I said, suddenly. Then I wrote it on my pad and held it up so she could see the crucial addition of the second *p.* "*Karen Lipps.*"

The morning after my date at the Waldorf, I was still obsessing about how I had nothing as I walked through Washington Square Park on my way to the office to put a few hours of work in before the nightmarish days ahead. Fashion

Week—when New York was transformed even more into Style Ground Zero than it already was by bringing in designers and models and scary thin rich people from around the city and around the world for shows and benefits and cocktail parties and dinners—was less than twenty-four hours away. I had a million things to do. Most of which—or all of which, actually—had to do with making sure nothing went wrong.

Please.

Like I cared.

The day before, a four-year-old had, in so many words, pointed out that my life was empty. So suddenly the idea of making sure six hundred press kits previewing our spring line got into the right hands made me want to shoot myself.

Anyway, there I was, on that beautiful September morning, wanting to shoot myself, when I saw a woman pushing a baby carriage. She was tall and thin with long perfect legs coming out of khaki shorts and as she stopped and knelt down to reposition a stuffed animal, I couldn't help but parse her outfit:

Karen Lipps front-pleat khaki walking shorts.

CK oversized charcoal cotton sweater.

DKNY black micro-fiber tote.

All-Star Converse high-tops in red canvas.

But when she stood up, turned around, and revealed the shit-eating grin of a blissfully happy new mother, I knew immediately that I had seen that smile before. I just couldn't remember where.

And then it came to me.

High school.

At seventeen, Marian Abrams was everything I was not. And now, given the child in the stroller, at thirty-three she was obviously *still* everything I was not.

Back then, she was one of the most attractive girls in the school.

I was not.

She was athletic.

I was not.

She was popular.

I was not.

She went to all the proms.

I didn't go to any of the proms.

She was dating the cutest nicest smartest boy in the school—the captain of the soccer team—who she had been dating since eighth grade. At the end of senior year they were both headed off to Princeton. And then, of course, they would get married and live happily ever after.

I was not.

I did not.

And, so far, I had not.

As you can see, I'd really made a lot of progress since the insecurity of my teens.

I edged over beside a tree and froze.

I hated moments like this.

To say hello or not to say hello. That was always the question.

Finally, something—perhaps the baby—perhaps the fact that I knew, given my state of mind that particular day, that I couldn't take another person asking me if I had a hud-band—tipped the scale of indecision and made me edge over a little farther to make my escape.

But that was not to be.

"*Ellen?*"

I froze again.

"*Ellen Franck?*"

I stared at her and feigned surprise, as if I hadn't been caught trying to sneak away into a hedge. "Marian . . . ?" I started. "Marian . . ."

"Abrams."

"Marian Abrams." I nodded hazily. "Of course."

"Rosalyn High School."

"Of *course*."

Don't remind me.

"Fifteen years," she said, her huge perfect teeth glowing as if the sun were a giant blue light that made everything already white even whiter. "You look great. And you still have great hair." She rolled her eyes to call my attention to her short straight brown hair. "I always envied your hair."

Marian Abrams used to envy my hair? I was shocked. Still, I couldn't resist pulling it out from the sides of my head like Bozo. "But *you* were the one with the perfect hair." I let the hair drop and then tried, unsuccessfully, to comb my fingers through it. "*You* were the one with *wings!*" I said *you* as if I were accusing her of something heinous.

I was, actually. A happy adolescence.

She rolled her eyes again. "Yours is thick. Mine's too thin. Not to mention the bald spot."

I stared at her as she pointed to the front of her head, just above and to the right of her forehead.

"*Bald,*" she said, giggling. "Bald, bald, *bald.*"

I almost liked her right then and there.

Who would have believed!

Marian Abrams going bald and making fun of herself!

But then I remembered.

The boyfriend.

The one from high school.

The one who was going to go to medical school and become an ob/gyn.

The oppressive weight and opacity of loserdom enveloped me as I imagined their perfect life together:

His Park Avenue practice; the pregnant women coming and going all day long.

Their huge fabulous apartment in a nearby doorman building, complete with FAO Schwartz-equipped nursery.

Her weekly pedicures and manicures.

The live-in nanny who was obviously off on Sundays.

It was time to cut this conversation short.

But somehow I couldn't.

I couldn't take my eyes off the bundle of cuteness in the carriage.

"Great baby," I said, despite myself, shifting the strap of my Karen Lipps black leather zip-tote on to my other shoulder.

"Thanks."

"How old is she?"

"Eight months."

Eight months.

Walking?

Maybe.

Talking?

Probably not.

Toilet trained?

Definitely not.

I wasn't really sure, actually. My sister and The Pickle lived in New England, which made it impossible for me to acquire the knowledge of a child's day-to-day minutiae first-hand. "You must be thrilled."

"We are."

We. Asshole. "Do you . . ."

"Stay home with her full time? No. We have a nanny."

"A nanny? Wow. That's great." Of course. Her husband's baby business was evidently booming.

"Well, I mean, she's full time but she doesn't live in."

I nodded, then stared admiringly in silence at the baby.

She cleared her throat. "So, do you . . . ?"

"Have one? No." *Not unless you count The Pickle.* I fell silent for a few seconds, then blurted out before I could stop myself. "But I really want one."

"I know," Marian said, nodding. I couldn't tell if the expression on her face was pity or self-satisfied smugness, but whatever it was I suddenly wanted to get away from it—and her.

"Well, listen," I said, reigning in the initial warmth I'd stupidly let fly because of her female-pattern baldness, "I've got to run." Then I mumbled something—*big job, big week, big big big life*—and put my KLNY sunglasses back on.

"Speaking of which, what do you do?" Marian asked.

I lit a cigarette and held it away from the baby carriage. "I work for Karen Lipps. P.R. Director." I exhaled dramatically and ran my hand luxuriously through my thick hair. So what if I were running out of eggs. At least I had a *job*. And hair.

"You're kidding," she said.

I exhaled again. "Why?"

She laughed. "I work for Calvin Klein. In-house counsel."

"Wait," I said, completely confused and extremely pissed off. "You're a *lawyer*?"

"What, you hate lawyers?"

"No," I said. "It's just that . . . well, I just thought that . . . you know, what with a baby and all, you probably wouldn't —"

She waited for me to finish my sentence, but I didn't. At least not audibly.

Since you were lucky enough to have a baby, I didn't think you would also be lucky enough to have a big job.

Marian suddenly looked uncomfortable, as if she, too, had had enough of this conversation, confirming my belief that high school is a time and a place that should never, ever be revisited.

"She's not mine." Marian blushed, then laughed guiltily. "She's my brother's."

I stared at her, overcome with enormous relief. Obviously, I was not the only loser here.

She smiled and bent down to make sure the baby was still sleeping. "Sometimes I just pretend she's mine."

"You *do*?" How weird was this?

"I mean, why is that so wrong?" she said, looking around the park and grinning without a trace of guilt. "It's not like I do it with people I know. I just do it here. In the park. With strangers. And I don't even do it on purpose. Things just come out of my mouth and somehow, at the time, they seem —"

"True," I said. "I know. I do the same thing with my niece."

"No way."

"Way."

We stared at each other and smiled.

"So, whatever happened to . . . ?" I tried to remember the name of her boyfriend-husband, but nothing came to me.

"Peter?"

"Right."

"It's a long story," she said, shaking her head. "What about you? Any potential—"

"Sperm donors? No. Not really." I sighed. "It's a long story, too."

It was always a long story.

"So, we should get together sometime," I said. "Form our own Imaginary Mommy Group."

"I could get a sitter."

"Or we could just double up on your nanny."

She laughed and reached into her bag to get out her datebook. "This is hell-week, though."

"I know," I said, flipping through my datebook, too. After going through about twenty-three possible lunch-drinks-dinner dates, we finally settled on one—dinner, on a Thursday, three weeks hence.

"By the way," I said, "do you like your job?"

"No," she said. "Do you like yours?"

"No."

We smirked and exchanged cards.

I knew then that we were destined to finally become friends.

Close friends.

BESTSELLING ARROW FICTION

☐ Night Shall Overtake Us	Kate Saunders	£6.99
☐ Wild Young Bohemians	Kate Saunders	£5.99
☐ Lily-Josephine	Kate Saunders	£5.99
☐ A Song For Summer	Eva Ibbotson	£5.99
☐ Seesaw	Deborah Moggach	£5.99
☐ Close Relations	Deborah Moggach	£5.99
☐ The Stainless Angel	Elizabeth Palmer	£5.99
☐ Plucking the Apple	Elizabeth Palmer	£5.99
☐ Old Money	Elizabeth Palmer	£5.99
☐ Flowering Judas	Elizabeth Palmer	£5.99
☐ The Golden Rule	Elizabeth Palmer	£5.99
☐ A Price For Everything	Mary Sheepshanks	£5.99
☐ Facing the Music	Mary Sheepshanks	£5.99
☐ Picking up the Pieces	Mary Sheepshanks	£5.99

ALL BOOKS ARE AVAILABLE THROUGH MAIL ORDER OR FROM YOUR LOCAL BOOKSHOP AND NEWSAGENT.

PLEASE SEND CHEQUE/EUROCHEQUE/POSTAL ORDER (STERLING ONLY) ACCESS, VISA, MASTERCARD, DINERS CARD, SWITCH OR AMEX.

☐☐☐☐☐☐☐☐☐☐☐☐☐☐☐☐

EXPIRY DATE ....SIGNATURE ....

PLEASE ALLOW 75 PENCE PER BOOK FOR POST AND PACKING U.K.

OVERSEAS CUSTOMERS PLEASE ALLOW £1.00 PER COPY FOR POST AND PACKING.

ALL ORDERS TO:

RANDOM HOUSE, BOOK SERVICE BY POST, TBS LIMITED, THE BOOK SERVICE, COLCHESTER ROAD, FRATING GREEN, COLCHESTER, ESSEX CO7 TDW.

NAME ....

ADDRESS ....

....

Please allow 28 days for delivery. Please tick box if you do not wish to receive any additional information ☐

Prices and availability subject to change without notice.